"You're Rosemarie, right?" Elijah asked.

The little girl nodded, moving toward her mother one slow, agonizing step at a time. She eyed him as if he was a coiled rattlesnake. Her hand stayed on the railing. The wall behind her was covered with photos.

Sweat broke out across Elijah's body.

His daughter was five. The family had to hate that their only surviving child had married an alcoholic. He had a lot to prove, but first he wanted to see his daughter smile. He lowered himself to a crouch so he wouldn't tower over her.

Finally, she made it to her mother's side and wrapped an arm around Jazmine's jean-clad leg.

"Hi, Rosemarie." He tried again, making sure to give her an easy smile. "I'm…" *Your dad, father, daddy.* Each word clogged his throat. None of them sounded right. "I'm so happy to meet you."

"You're my daddy, right?" Her tiny, bow-shaped lips twisted to the side.

He couldn't b

A seventh-generation Texan, **Jolene Navarro** fills her life with family, faith and life's beautiful messiness. She knows that as much as the world changes, people stay the same: vow-keepers and heartbreakers. Jolene married a vow-keeper who shows her holding hands never gets old. When not writing, Jolene teaches art to inner-city teens and hangs out with her own four almost-grown kids. Find Jolene on Facebook or her blog, jolenenavarrowriter.com.

Books by Jolene Navarro

Love Inspired

Lone Star Legacy

Texas Daddy
The Texan's Twins
Lone Star Christmas

Lone Star Holiday
Lone Star Hero
A Texas Christmas Wish
The Soldier's Surprise Family
The Texan's Secret Daughter

Love Inspired Historical

Lone Star Bride

The Texan's Secret Daughter

Jolene Navarro

HARLEQUIN® LOVE INSPIRED®

 LOVE INSPIRED BOOKS

Recycling programs
for this product may
not exist in your area.

ISBN-13: 978-1-335-53925-0

The Texan's Secret Daughter

www.Harlequin.com

Printed in U.S.A.

Peace I leave with you, my peace I give unto you: not as the world giveth, give I unto you. Let not your heart be troubled, neither let it be afraid.
—*John* 14:27

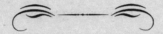

To Andrea Porter. She might not be a writer, but she has created an oasis for writers in Canyon, Texas. The West Texas Writer's Academy is one of the highlights of my year. Thank you.

Acknowledgments

The West Texas Bangers—
C.S. Kjar, Jenna Neal, Kimberly Packard, Lana Pattinson, Linda Fry and Linda Trout, for helping me through the twists and turns of Elijah and Jazmine's journey to their happy-ever-after. See you in June.

Pam Hopkins—
the best agent a girl could wish for.

Emily Rodmell—
I've said it before but it's true. My stories are better because of your insight and knowledge.

Chapter One

No. That couldn't be him.

Jazmine Daniels stood in the doorway of the food bank. The bags loaded with canned goods cut into her fingers, but she couldn't move. She understood now why deer froze in the middle of the road.

Walk in, turn around, run, hide.

The options tumbled over each other in her brain, confusing her body and making it impossible to pick one.

Elijah De La Rosa. It had been over six years since she'd seen her husband. Ex-husband.

His hair was a little longer and there was more red tangled in the dark strands, as though he'd spent a lot of time outdoors. He looked older, his skin weathered in a good way. A small groan formed in the back of her throat. How was it possible that he was even better looking now than the day she had first seen him? Not fair.

He laughed at something one of his companions said, and she forced herself to look away. Her mother and daughter would be following her any minute. She needed to leave before that happened.

Her eyes scanned the large open room for a fast escape. Colorful carved starfish hung on the walls while windows flooded the dining area with friendly sunlight. About twenty-five people gathered around the long tables, eating the lunch that the local mission provided to the homeless and needy.

Homeless? Her stomach plunged. He couldn't be homeless, but why else would he be here? The drinking must've gotten worse after she left. Had his family refused to help him or had he refused to accept their help?

His pride had always been bigger than his common sense. Not that she had blamed him. Her heart had wanted to fix all his hurts, but she hadn't been enough.

She shook her head and bit hard against the remorse. No. Her actions kept her and her daughter safe. That had to stay at the forefront of her brain.

The good times wanted to sneak in and melt

her heart for the boy she had loved with every fiber of her being. That boy was long gone.

This was the reason her mother had told her to stay away from their beach home. Both of her parents had agreed that any kind of contact was dangerous for her. They had handled everything needed for the divorce.

She hadn't seen him again, only his signature on the papers that broke the vows they had made to each other.

No, *he* had broken those vows. She glanced down at the ugly white scar running from her palm to the underside of her wrist. It had been caused by her own careless mistake, but it was a was a tangible reminder of that night.

The night she had come face-to-face with the ugly truth of his self-destruction.

He had never hurt her, physically or emotionally, but his hatred of the world leaked into all his actions.

When her heart's memory failed her, one glance at the mark reinforced why she had left. He had refused her help and closed her out.

Her daughter's safety had been her priority. So, she had run from him without saying a word about the pregnancy.

Guilt was hard to live with. This last year, she had almost called him several times. Rosemarie had asked about her father. With first grade starting in the fall, it was time to let Elijah know about their daughter.

But only if he was sober. She refused to put Rosemarie in danger.

Eyes burning, she took a step back. This was not how she had imagined their first meeting. In a homeless shelter. Beautiful, proud Elijah with the quick and easy smile was eating a free lunch at a homeless shelter.

She glanced at the door. It wasn't that far. She looked back at him, then groaned. Too late. They had made eye contact. Her lack of decision had taken the choice out of her hand.

His eyes lifted, and the smile that used to make her heart flutter slipped into a frown. He tilted his head, as if he couldn't figure out what he was looking at.

The exit was just a few feet away. Maybe she could rewind, go right out the front and pretend she hadn't seen him. Her breathing came faster. Her feet were cemented to the cold floor.

"Jazz?" It sounded as though his throat was full of sand.

He stood. A worn T-shirt with the words Saltwater Cowboys stretched across his broad chest. There was a rip at the neckline.

One, two, three slow steps and he was

around the table. Then he stopped, like he was afraid of getting too close.

His faded jeans were low on his hips and fit him perfectly, but they were threadbare and ripped at the knees. Small flecks of paint decorated the denim. Was he painting houses now, or were they secondhand clothes?

After growing up in hand-me-downs from church donations, Elijah had refused to wear anything someone else had thrown away. He'd started working at thirteen. Once he had a job, he had dressed immaculately every day, his boots constantly polished.

Even on his worst days, he'd still looked put together. Until he stumbled through the door late at night, drunk.

She lowered her eyes. Those boots looked worse for wear.

"Jazmine? What are you doing here?" Two more steps brought him close enough for her to see the unusual blend of color in his eyes. The color of Spanish moss, somewhere between gray and green. The exact shade of her daughter's.

Unable to talk, she lifted the bags of food she, her mother and daughter had brought in to donate. To her horror, her arms started shaking.

"Here, let me get those for you." He reached

over and took the bags, his callused hands brushing her wrist. His fingers touched her scar and she jumped back, ripping one of the bags and sending cans rolling over the floor.

The men who had been sitting with him rushed to help pick up the canned vegetables and junk food her mother had cleaned out of the beach house's pantry.

After a bit of fumbling and laughing, one of the older men brought a new bag, and they collected her donations.

"So, who's this lovely lady, Elijah?" The shortest one said with a grin. It was hard to judge their ages, due to the rough life that was written in every wrinkle and crease.

Elijah cleared his throat. "Guys, this is Jazmine…" He looked at her with a question in his eyes.

"Daniels. Jazmine Daniels." She couldn't look him in the eyes, afraid to see his reaction when she learned that she'd dropped his name. Holding out her now free hand, she made sure to smile. So, what if pieces of her world were crumbling around her? There was no need for them to know. "Pleasure to meet you. Thank you for the help."

They handed her the bags.

Her ex-husband started introducing the three

men, but they all went wide-eyed. "This is Jazmine? Your Jazz girl?"

His? Had he been talking about her to these men? Her forehead wrinkled as she glared at him.

He closed his eyes and grimaced.

When he reached for the bags this time, she was ready. She held her ground without acting like a middle-school girl at her first dance.

"The food donations go in the pantry area. Through the door over there." He pointed his chin to the left, then walked in that direction.

She followed without thinking but stopped midway. No way was she going anywhere with him. She glanced over her shoulder. Then again, he was leaving the dining area where her mother and daughter could appear any minute.

With a deep breath, she went through the swinging door. She'd get his number and get out before anyone was the wiser. Three women were working behind the counter. Jazmine recognized two of them from the summers she'd spent at the beach. Their eyes went wide when they saw her.

"Well, I'll be. Jazmine Daniels De La Rosa, it's been ages." Kate glanced at Elijah, then back to Jazmine. "This is quite the surprise. So, what are you doing in Foster?"

"I'm at Port Del Mar with my parents. We're staying at the beach house, so my father can recover."

The other woman, Martha, nodded. "Sorry to hear about what happened. Y'all brought him to the right place to recover. The beach is so much better than that city. The salt air at Port D has healing powers. We'll keep him in our prayers. You should take him over—"

"Martha." Kate shook her head. "She's not here to jibber jabber." Smiling at Jazmine, she took the bags. "Interesting that you and Elijah brought these donations in together. We haven't seen you in what? Over six years? Your parents don't come as often, either." The women glanced between her and Elijah, waiting for an explanation.

Obviously, Kate wanted to talk as much as Martha. The news of her being in Port Del Mar with Elijah would be flying as if a town crier was dashing up and down the boardwalk. Another reason she should get out of here.

The way Elijah found out about Rosemarie needed to be well planned. The gossip mill was not how a man should discover he was the father of a five-year-old girl.

Elijah gave in to the silent pressure first. "I was as surprised as you when she walked in the door. I was just helping with the bags. Nothing interesting here."

"That's sweet of you." Martha looked as if she was about to ask more questions, but Kate interrupted her.

"Well, we need to take these to the back and start the dishes. Y'all have a good one. Tell your parents hi and that they're in our prayers."

They all smiled at Elijah as if he was a favorite son. Then they disappeared through the back door.

It shouldn't have surprised her that they still adored him, even if he had fallen on hard times. Despite his uncle's reputation in town as a mean drunk and cheat, Elijah had charmed everyone. Except for his uncle and Jazmine's parents.

She blamed his uncle for teaching him the family tradition of drinking. But then her parents had made his life even harder. They had all had a hand in destroying their marriage.

Shaking her head, she cleared her thoughts. They might have made his life difficult, but she had promised to quit making excuses for him. He made his choices, and she was not going to feel guilty. She wasn't.

And if she said that enough maybe she'd believe it.

His decision to turn to the bottle instead of

to her and God had been his alone. Elijah had put an end to their happily-ever-after. There was no going back once trust was lost.

He turned to her and ran his long fingers through his hair. He focused on the counter, not making eye contact.

"Well, by dinnertime everyone in Port Del Mar will know you're back and that we were seen together." Finally, he looked at her. The corner of his mouth twitched.

Her stupid heart fluttered and skipped a beat.

He took a step closer. "It's amazing that you're here. I was going to try to contact your parents again. I really have to talk to you."

Her heart hit her ribs in double time. Had he found out about Rosemarie?

He stared at her for a long, silent moment, then gave her that old half smile he used whenever he thought he was in trouble. Unfortunately, it had worked way too many times.

She had a long track record of giving in to his promises, promises that never survived forty-eight hours.

She was stronger now. Straightening her spine, she made sure to look him right in the eyes. "What is it, Elijah?"

Something on his fingernail became the center of his world.

"Elijah, I have to go, but if you give me your number, I'll call and we can…talk."

He took a deep breath and nodded. "I've practiced this speech for years, and now that you're standing in front of me all the words have disappeared. Jazz, you're the only person left on my list that I need to apologize to."

She frowned. "List?" Then she understood. "You're doing the twelve steps?"

Scrutinizing his features, she looked for any clue that he was lying. Would she be able to tell if he was sober?

He nodded as he stuffed his hands into the front pockets of those worn jeans. "Yeah. I started it a few years back, but well… I haven't been able to reach you. And I…"

"Momma! Look what GiGi got me!" Rosemarie, her five-year-old daughter—*their* five-year-old daughter—rushed through the doorway, holding up a fragile-looking doll in a Victorian dress and oversize hat.

Jazmine looked over her daughter's shoulder but didn't see her mother. Yet. "That's lovely, sweetheart. Can you go wait with GiGi for a minute? I need to take care of some business."

"But I thought we were going to—"

"Jazmine?" Behind her, Elijah's voice was even rougher than before. She dropped her head and shut her eyes. Putting a hand on Rosemarie's tiny shoulder, she turned to face him.

"Elijah. We need to talk—"

"Obviously." The word was barely audible through his clenched teeth.

The clicking of heels on the concrete flooring told her that time was up. Her mother was going to take this stressful moment up another level. It was like watching a collision about to happen in slow motion and not being able to stop it.

Gasps sounded at the doorway. "Jazmine. What is going on?"

Calming her mind, she waited a few seconds before turning to her mother with a smile on her face. "Mother, you remember Elijah?" She glanced at Rosemarie, hoping Azalea would take the hint. "He was having lunch and offered to help me with our donations."

"Jazmine, this is exactly why I told you to stay away." Azalea Daniels pinned a hard glare on Elijah. In a few quick steps, she had Rosemarie's hand in hers. She pulled the little girl closer to her side, staring Elijah down. "You're eating lunch at the food bank? Did you lose your home, too? Homeless. It shouldn't surprise me."

"Mother! Not helping." Jazmine rubbed her

temple. A massive headache was climbing into her frontal lobe.

With an indignant nod, Azalea dropped her gaze to the five-year-old. "Papa is waiting. The nurse will be leaving soon, and I must talk to her." She gave a tight nod to Elijah before heading to the door. When Jazmine didn't immediately follow, her mother's spine stiffened. "Jazmine?"

"Mom, take Rosemarie to the car. I'll be right there, I promise." She made a point of looking at the innocent little girl standing there without a clue of the drama swirling around her. "Please."

"Two minutes." With tight lips and one last warning glare, Azalea walked out the door.

"That's my daughter. You—"

"Yes, she's your daughter and we need to talk."

"You not only left me without a word, but you took my daughter?" He stared at the door Rosemarie had just walked through, his chest rising and falling in rapid movements. "I have a daughter." He turned to her, eyes flashing intense heat. "Your parents knew. They knew."

"Yes. Like I said, we need to talk. I have to go right now, but I can meet you tomorrow—"

"Tonight. We'll meet tonight or I'm camping at the beach house door until we talk."

"Don't come to the house. That would upset Daddy, and we have to keep him calm. I'll meet you tonight at Pier 19. We can grab some coffee. Is the Painted Dolphin still there?" That was probably a mistake. Every wall was covered with memories of when they were dating and the early days of their marriage. The days that were filled with joy and laughter. When they thought they could conquer the world with their love.

The last thing she needed right now was all the could-have-beens from the good days before the drinking started.

He snorted. "Yeah, it's there. New owners reopened it last month." A grim expression shifted across his face. "What's going on with your father?"

"He suffered a heart attack while driving and crashed his car and wanted to recover at the beach house."

Elijah frowned. "I'm sorry. I know how close you are to your father. Is he going to be okay?"

"The heart attack itself was minor as far as these things go, but he was also injured when he hit a street sign. It didn't yield." She held back a groan. *Not an appropriate time for humor, Jazmine.* "Anyway, if we can convince him to follow doctor's orders, he'll recover fully." The acid in her stomach started climbing up her throat. "I also came because I knew it was time for us to come together and discuss a few things."

"Really? A few things?" he snarled at her. "About six years too late."

She took a step back. "This isn't something that can be done over the phone. I wanted to see how you were and…" She cut her glance back to the dining area. "I was hoping you were…"

"Sober?" His nostrils flared, a clear sign he was angry. "I've been sober for five years now."

Her eyes closed. If that was true, she didn't want to think about the time she wasted worrying about calling him. "I was hoping you were better. I didn't mean to meet you like this or for you to see her for the first time without…" She fluttered her hand helplessly in front of her, then looked at her bare wrist as though there was a watch there. The glimpse of her scar gave her new resolve, and she became businesslike once more. "I need to go. Rosemarie goes to bed at 8:30. I'll see you at nine?"

"Rosemarie? You named her Rosemarie De La Rosa?"

"She's Rosemarie Daniels. I did want Rose in her name, and since my mother's family has a history of naming the girls after flowers, I thought…" She needed to stop babbling.

His eyes went dark and hard. She took another step back. That was the expression of rage she had learned to fear. He had never deliberately hurt her, but that look had always made her wonder if the potential was there.

"Does she even know about me? Does she know who her father is?"

"Yes. She knows your name." Today he didn't resemble that boy at all. "How long have you been at the shelter? Never mind. I'm sorry. I need to go. I promise I'll answer all your questions tonight. And don't worry about the tab. I'll cover it."

He leaned back on the counter. For a second, he closed his eyes. He inhaled deeply, causing his chest to expand. When he finally looked at her, the flash of anger was gone, but his face was closed and hard to read. "I can afford a couple of cups of coffee."

He smiled, the kind of smile that was a bit forced. Like he had to remind himself to play nice. It showed off the long dimple on his left cheek, and the new lines at the corner of his eyes. "I'll even throw in some sopaipillas. I could actually get you one of everything on the menu if you want. I have an in with the chef."

"I'm sorry. I didn't mean to insult you. I

just—" This was so much worse than she had feared. *God, please lead me in this and give me the words and strength I need to make this right for everyone.*

He straightened and walked toward her. When she backed away from him, he stopped and frowned. "Why are you acting as if you're afraid of me? I never hurt you." His hard gaze held her in place, studying her like an image he couldn't identify. "Did I?"

Forcing herself to stand still, she shook her head. "No. You never hurt me. I'm sorry." Why was she apologizing?

"Don't worry about it. It takes a lot more these days to upset me. Just be there." Each word clipped and tense. "If you're not, expect me at the house. I'll stand at the door until you answer."

Her phone vibrated. She glanced down and saw her mother's name. "I've gotta go."

"Jazz?"

His low voice made her knees weak. She could not afford to be weak. "Don't call me that. I'm not that naive girl anymore."

"You'll be there?"

"I'm not the one who breaks promises." With resolve, she pivoted and headed for the door.

"No, you only hide a child from her father."

She almost stumbled. That was a punch to

the gut. And the worst part? He was right. And he had every right to be angry. But she was not going to regret what she did to keep her daughter safe. Not looking at him, she replied, "I'll be there. I'm also going to do whatever it takes to keep her safe."

Then she rushed out of the pantry area. Now she was going to have to explain all this to her daughter.

Chapter Two

Standing alone, Elijah tried to clear his brain. The hum of the commercial refrigerators gave him something safe to focus on, anything other than the curve of her face. The rust colored freckles that dusted her cheeks over soft mahogany skin. The need to reach out and touch her, to make sure she was real had been a punch to the gut. He buried his fingers in his hair and dropped his head.

For over five years, he had practiced his apology, holding each word tightly in his mind until the day he could tell her. He had written letter after letter, flooding her parents' mailbox with them. Not that she had seen any of them—her parents had made that clear—but he had been desperate to make things right. And now the day had come, and he hadn't uttered a word of his apology. He'd blown it. Anger soured his stomach.

Because she had stolen his child. Digging his fingers into his scalp, he dropped into a crouch, elbows dug into his knees. Did she actually believed he was homeless? He laughed. Alone in the pantry, he laughed out loud.

And then he stopped. Took a few deep breaths. Right now, he needed to be calm and steady. He couldn't afford to lose his grip.

The Daniels were powerful people in the state of Texas. Elijah couldn't imagine Judge Nelson James Daniels III ever being weak. The man ruled his world with an iron fist. There was only one person Elijah knew with a stronger will—Azalea Daniels, his wife, Jazmine's mother. She and her husband had hated him from the first moment he had stepped on their porch to take their daughter to a beach party to kick off the summer season.

He was only two years older, but at the time, his twenty to Jazmine's eighteen was too big of a gap for them. He wasn't in school or planning to attend. Plus, they knew his uncle.

Frank had stood in front of Judge Daniels's bench more times than Elijah wanted to think about.

The Daniels family had faced their own tragedy, losing a young son to a drunk driver. Elijah was an idiot. Leaning his forehead against the door, he planted his fist against the wall. This was 100 percent his fault. Why had he tried to overstep and reach for something he didn't deserve?

With his program and counseling, he'd finally been in a place to let it go, to let her go. Making amends and apologizing was all he'd had left, but everything had just changed.

Jazmine, the Daniels's only surviving child, had had a bright future. Even before her senior year had started, she had been accepted to three Ivy League schools on the East Coast. Elijah, on the other hand, had barely gotten out of high school.

He preferred the outdoors. On a horse, working with cattle, or on a boat out in the Gulf fighting the elements. Both of those were a thousand times more fulfilling than sitting behind a desk at the job Judge Daniels had gotten him.

He closed his eyes. That job had taken all the life out of him, but instead of talking he had started drinking.

Needless to say, her parents had not been happy when Jazmine had decided to stay and attend the local college, so she could stay close to him. They had done everything but disown her when they had gotten married.

Then his stupid De La Rosa weakness had to ruin it all, giving her parents the perfect opportunity to take her away from him.

He had never hurt Jazmine. Not physically. A hollow thud hit his gut. At least, he didn't think he had.

The night she had left was a foggy mess of impressions. No matter how hard he focused, that night, like so many others, was a blur. All he remembered was the bang of the thunder and blinding flashes of lightning.

When he had woken up, she had been gone and had never returned. Until today.

The huge ornate mirror her parents had given them had been smashed into hundreds of razor-sharp shards. There had been traces of blood on both the frame and his knuckles. He hoped the glass was the only thing he had broken. The thought of touching her in anger made him sick to his stomach. Even at his worst, he wouldn't do that. Would he?

The token in his pocket had a strip of paper wrapped around it. He pulled it out. This morning his meditation verse had been Second Corinthians 5:17. *Old things are passed away; behold, all thing are becoming new.*

When he had read his daily meditation scripture before the sun had risen over the

Gulf this morning, God knew what this day would bring.

One of the first lessons he'd had to learn was that in order to control his life, he had to control his anger. Getting angry was never going to help. He had to focus on today and what he needed to do going forward.

He wanted to show Jazmine that they had all been wrong about him. He had become a successful businessman. Just a few months ago, he and his partner had added the Painted Dolphin to their line of restaurants here along the coast. They just added another boat to their recreational fleet. With God, he had become a new man.

Becoming new. But, boy, did that take on new meaning today. Elijah closed his eyes and rubbed the sobriety token between his thumb and index finger.

If he was going to get through this day, he couldn't go into the past. It would be like those long lines of dominoes he had loved setting up as a kid. One negative thought would trigger another until a tidal wave of guilt sucked him under. The alcohol used to help him silence the voices, but he couldn't give in now. He couldn't go back to that dark place.

There was a little girl who needed a sober father. The man he had been for the last five years could be that father. He would give her what his uncle had never given him.

Anger flared again. They had stolen five years of his daughter's life from him. Elijah took out his phone and called his best friend and business partner. One of the people who had helped him stay sober.

"Hey, Miguel. I need to talk."

"What's up?" The casual question was lined with concern. A door closed and the background noise vanished.

Elijah knew he had his friend's full attention. His throat went dry. He couldn't believe the words he was about to say.

"I just saw Jazmine. She's in town."

"Oh, wow. That had to be a surprise." There was a short pause, as though Miguel was struggling for words. "How are you doing?"

"That's not all." He took a deep breath. "I'm a father. She was pregnant when she left. I have a five-year-old daughter."

Silence fell.

"Miguel?"

"Yeah, I'm here. You didn't have a clue?"

"Nope." Suddenly his throat burned, and he beat back the tears. "I know I have to take responsibility because my drinking drove her away from me. She couldn't trust me, and she thought she was protecting our baby. But

Miguel, every time I think about what I've missed the last five years, I want to explode. I'm not sure I've ever been this angry at someone, not even my mother or uncle."

"Yeah, losing people is one of the reasons you stopped drinking, right? So the people you love can trust you. I have to say you also have a right to be angry, but that's not going to help. Are you at the ranch? I can be out there in the next fifteen minutes."

"No, I'm at the mission. I'll come to the pier. Are you there?"

"Yep. Come straight over, okay? I'll be waiting."

"I won't stop." Elijah disconnected the call. *Lord, You've gotten me through the darkest times. I trust You have a plan in all this. Give me the wisdom to know the right thing to do and the patience to wait for Your timing.*

He was going to need more wisdom and patience than he'd ever thought possible.

On the drive back to Port Del Mar, Rosemarie had chatted away about her new doll and the horse she wanted to get her. All her dolls had their own horses. She was oblivious to the silent tension between her mother and grandmother.

Driving down Shoreline Road, Jazmine

didn't even take the time to appreciate the beautiful beach that lined the tiny coastal town. There were two main roads that ran parallel to each other. In some spots, the strip of land between the bay and the Gulf was less than a mile wide.

Her father had inherited the beachfront home that had been a staple of Jazmine's childhood. It was one of her favorite places on Earth. But her parents had kept her away since that night, not allowing her anywhere near Port Del Mar.

It had been six long years since the sounds of the waves and the feel of the salty breeze filled her senses.

This was her daughter's first trip to Texas.

She pulled into the long, bricked driveway lined with tall palm trees and large fuchsia flowers. The soft blue house trimmed in pristine white stood three stories tall. By the time Jazmine parked in the carport, Rosemarie was climbing out of her booster seat.

"Momma, unlock the door so I can show Becca to Papa."

"Remember he needs to be resting." She turned to her daughter. "Don't wake him if he's asleep. Can you be quiet?"

Rosemarie's dark curls bounced as she nodded. "I can be as quiet as a mouse." In a heartbeat, she jumped out of the SUV and leaped up the stairs.

Jazmine waited for her daughter to disappear inside the house before turning to her mother. "Thank you for not making a scene in front of Rosie. Go ahead. Out with it. What have you been champing at the bit to tell me?"

"First, I don't champ. Second, this is a mistake. She does not need that man in her life. You need to pack up and go back to Denver." Azalea's arms were crossed, and her face was set like stone.

"His name is Elijah. Not saying his name will not make him go away. She's his daughter. The least I can do is talk to him."

Jazmine looked at the organized walls of the garage. Everything fit in a perfect space. If it didn't, it was tossed out. No room for anything undesirable. "I'm not leaving you alone with Daddy. He's not a good patient. In less than a week, he will drive you crazy. You need me as much as he needs you. With Rosie around, he might be easier to handle."

"There is nothing easy about your father." The perfectly lined lip quivered.

Jazmine reached across and placed her hand over her mother's. "He's going to be fine. Dr. Brent feels good about a full recovery. It is going to take all of us to keep him from overdoing it. I'm not going anywhere. I can be just as stubborn as you."

With a harsh exhalation, her mother rolled her eyes. "You get that from your father. We can't tell him that Rosie...that...her father..." She shuddered. "I just don't like this. What if he causes problems? He was always good at that."

"Mother, what we did was wrong. He had every right to know about Rosemarie. I know I had to leave, but we should have told him." She pressed one arm over her middle, trying to ease the sick feeling. "I have to meet him. We should have never done it."

"Your father and I did exactly what we needed to do to keep our daughter and our granddaughter safe. I would do it all over again, with not a single regret." She rubbed the edge of her purse.

"That night you came to us, you were so scared, and you had that nasty cut. I can't get the blood-soaked towel you had wrapped around your arm out of my head. There is no reason for me to say his name." Her shoulders squared.

"I told you. He never hurt me. I got cut trying to pick up the shards of glass. My hands were shaking." Jazmine relaxed her grip on the steering wheel, revealing her scar again.

"If you had been able to stop us from getting married, we wouldn't have Rosemarie."

Azalea sighed and dropped her head. "Okay, so I wouldn't change that part. But I would still send you and Rosie away. I'm not sure I believe the story about the glass. You had a habit of making excuses for him."

She dug into her purse and pulled out her gold tube of lipstick. Lowering the visor, she used the mirror to reapply the bronze color. "Sweetheart, it doesn't look good. I mean we found him eating lunch at Esperanza's Kitchen. You know that's for homeless people. He's fallen further than even I would have guessed."

Jazmine wanted to beat her head against the windshield. "We don't know why he was there. His family still owns the Diamondback Ranch."

"His family might own land, but they have major issues. If he's been kicked out of that family, he's really sunk low. You shouldn't go alone. We'll arrange to have him come to the law office. He can be reminded who he's up against."

"No. I'm not going to have this turn into a legal battle. That would just drag it out. Rosie doesn't deserve a messy court battle between her parents."

"What if he hasn't changed?"

Jazmine took a moment to stifle the words she wanted to scream at her mother. "Rosemarie's older. She'll be able to call me if she needs to. She—"

"You're not going to let him be alone with her!"

"Not right now, but when she's older. Keeping them apart is wrong."

"What he put you through was wrong. What would you do if Rosie was in the same situation?"

Jazmine bit her lips to hold in words of frustration. There was really no arguing with her parents. "They don't know each other, so any meetings we set up now will be with me. I'm not going to just drop her off with a stranger and leave."

"We need to get something in writing, some sort of legal agreement before you allow him to talk to her. We have to protect her and make sure he can't—"

Jazmine's fist hit the steering wheel. "Stop. She has as much right to know about her father as he does to know about her. We're meeting tonight, and I'll make a plan from there." She twisted and faced her mother. "You're going to have to trust me on this. Okay?"

Her mother sighed. "I'm not sure I trust you when you're in the same room as him."

"That love-struck girl has grown up. I'm not going to allow anyone to hurt my daughter. If he is sober, we'll come up with a plan that protects her."

"If I can't change your mind, then please be careful. I don't want to see you hurt again. And you have to think about that innocent little girl." She looked out the window. "With your father down, I just can't…"

Jazmine reached across the center console and threaded her fingers through her mother's. "I know. But if nothing else, this has reminded me that our lives can change in a blink. I can't put this off any longer."

"Rosemarie is so trusting."

"I won't let anyone hurt her. That includes her father." She gave her mother a hard look. "And her grandparents. Have you thought about the questions she'll have in a few years when she learns we kept her father from her?"

With a quick nod and a deep sigh, Azalea got out of the car and headed for the stairs.

Jazmine rested her forehead on the steering wheel. Her heart wasn't so sure she would be fine with Elijah being in Rosemarie's life, but for her daughter's sake, she couldn't hide behind her parents any longer.

Elijah was going to find how much she'd changed. The meek girl was gone. She was a full-grown mama bear now, and if she thought he would hurt Rosemarie in any way, she was walking out. Even if she left behind another piece of her heart.

Chapter Three

Jazmine arrived at the Painted Dolphin thirty minutes early. She wanted to be there before Elijah so she could pick the table where this meeting would take place. The seat of power had to be hers. She walked around the building, then went up the steps.

A few boats with lights strung over every mast and piece of rigging sailed by in the bay. A longing surprised her.

A young staff member in a tie-dyed T-shirt came over to her. "Can I help you?"

A nervous laugh slipped out. Why did she felt like a teenager sneaking out of her parents' house? "Yes. I'm meeting someone." She scanned the large room. Several life-size sculpted dolphins painted with bright patterns still hung from the ceiling, but everything else looked new. The place was a surprising mix of modern and bohemian charm. Elijah had said it had been reopened a couple of months ago.

"Ma'am?" The blonde, sun-kissed girl looked at her with concern.

"Oh, I'm sorry. I use to come here all the time. It looks different."

She smiled. "It looks great, right? So, do you want to sit inside or on the deck? The singer will be starting up again, so if you want to talk, then I suggest the deck. Sitting by the water is nice. It's my favorite place."

Jazmine nodded. "I always sat next to the railing." She glanced across the room at the long wooden serving counter and froze. He was already here.

Working? He shook hands with someone and laughed.

Then he saw her and his smile vanished. With a few words to the man, he left the register area and headed straight for her. The work-worn clothes were gone. A blue dress shirt was open at the neck, the long sleeves rolled up to his elbows.

Oh my. The beach bum cowboy cleaned up well. Very well.

He moved with the easy grace she remembered from the early days. Like he owned everything around him. The confidence that he had shown the world was always in conflict with his self-esteem.

Without a doubt he had always been gorgeous, and she had never understood what he had seen in her. All the local girls had wondered the same thing. Her parents said he had just been after her money and social standing, but she had never believed that.

As she watched him, she saw a difference in him. He seemed more…more *something*. What, she wasn't sure, but wow. Okay, so it looked as if he had a steady job. That was good.

"Hey, Jenny. I'll seat Ms. Daniels."

"Hi, Mr. De La Rosa. Oh." She looked back to Jazmine. "You're meeting Mr. De La Rosa."

"Yes. She's meeting me. We're going to be outside at table seven. Will you bring us some chips with guacamole and some lemonade?"

"Of course, sir. I'll have it right out." Her long blond hair swung as she turned to do his bidding.

With his most charming wink, he grinned at her. "You're early."

Caught. She glanced around. "I wanted to—"

"Get here first to get the lay of the land." He chuckled. "I'm not surprised." He lifted his right arm and gestured to the doors leading out to the deck. "Ladies first."

She glanced around as they walked under the giant garage doors made of glass. Two of the three were rolled up into the ceiling, leaving the restaurant open to the water. On a small platform, a man was strumming a guitar and softly singing. The dining area looked busy. "Will you get in trouble for talking while you're at work?"

With a half-hearted chuckle, he shook his head. "No. I'm good. I'm pretty tight with the owner." He pushed back his hair.

Her brain was trying to catch up. The Elijah she saw this afternoon was not matching up with the Mr. De La Rosa she followed now. "You work here?" Was he the manager? "You're not...why were you eating at Esperanza's today?"

Outside, they walked to the far corner of the railed deck. He pulled out the chair on the opposite side of the table and waited for her to sit before seating himself across from her. "I volunteer there, and I have a few men there I visit with whenever I get the chance."

"Oh." Her cheeks felt warm. "Are they in AA?"

He gave her a tight smile. "We're here to talk about our daughter."

"Of course." Opening her purse, she pulled out an envelope. "I printed these up for you. I can send you more if you want."

His hands shook a little as he picked up the pictures. Was he nervous or was it a side effect from all the drinking? The gentle lapping of the water against the pier was the only sound as she watched him.

He flipped through the pictures one at a time, studying each one as if devouring every detail. They started with the first hospital pictures and ended with a selfie they had taken yesterday while waiting for the car to take them to the airport. He looked through them again.

The only indication of what he was feeling was the flicker of muscle on his jawline and the bounce of his Adam's apple. Unable to watch any longer, she let her gaze follow the boats in the harbor.

The clearing of his throat brought her attention back to him. He held the envelope out to her.

"No. Those are yours."

"Thanks." He slid them into his shirt pocket. For a moment his hand rested there.

Needing to focus on something else, her gaze swept their old hangout. "It's nice. I like the changes. How long have you worked here?"

"About six months." He sighed. His gaze darted around like he was embarrassed.

"You have the look of a manager." She tried to keep her face neutral, rather than judgmental, but she wasn't sure how successful she was. "So, you're not homeless? You run the restaurant? That's great."

He shifted to the side and opened his mouth, then clamped it shut.

There was something in his eyes that seemed off. Was he ashamed? "It's the perfect job for you. Outdoors, no sitting still. And you were always good with people. Working at a desk indoors everyday was not a good fit."

"What about you? Have you moved back to Texas for good?"

"No. I took family leave to help my mother. I'm an event planner for a large resort in Denver. I have eight weeks, and then we're going back."

"Eight weeks?" He popped his knuckles. "I have eight weeks to get to know her before you leave."

Nodding was all she could manage.

He leaned back, one arm draped across the empty chair next to his. The silky blue shirt pulled taut across his shoulders. He studied her, those intense gray eyes making her look away. She took in the boats. There were the normal charters and sailboats, but at the very end there was a new addition. A huge, old-fashioned ship bobbed in the water.

There had to be something safe she could talk about. "Is that a pirate ship?"

"Yeah. It's new. I've been out on it a few times. It's fun to watch it go by when I'm eating dinner on our deck at home."

Biting the inside of her lip, she shut her eyes. The little beachfront cottage they had bought in the first months of their marriage.

It was on the opposite side of town. Her parents had given them the down payment to the fixer-upper. She had loved that place. "Our deck? I thought the house was sold in the divorce."

"They didn't tell you anything, did they?" This time his look of disgust wasn't directed at her.

"No. They thought it would be easier for me." Why was she suddenly afraid to hear what had happened to their little home? They had worked so hard together to restore the beach cottage until it was just the way she wanted it.

"Originally, they told me to sell it." He shrugged. "I wanted to keep it. We had put so much sweat equity into it. It was the first time ever I had a real home." He took a drink of his lemonade. "It looked like I was going to lose again. I didn't have the money to buy you out." His fingers ran along the braided leather bracelet he wore on his left wrist. "Then the hurricane hit. There was a great deal of damage. We wouldn't have been able to sell anytime soon, so I made an offer to buy your half at a discount. My cousin Xavier helped me out. I still live there."

She wasn't sure why the idea of him fighting for their house made her heart flutter, but she needed to move on to other thoughts. "Were you able to rebuild?"

"I discovered that I have a skill for rebuilding."

She turned her attention to the busy restaurant. "You always enjoyed being out on the water. You talked about owning your own fishing boats."

He looked away and waved to some people on a boat gliding by. "I talked to my lawyer about child support. She's going to do some research and figure out how much I owe you."

"What?" The change of subject startled her. "No. I don't want your money. I'm fine."

His attention returned to her. Now his eyes were a steel gray. "It's not for you. I'm not a deadbeat dad."

"Elijah. You don't—"

His fist clenched. "I will not be my father."

He took a deep breath and relaxed into his chair. "Buy her shoes or a pony or put it aside for college. I don't want her to ever think I didn't support her." He pulled a card out of his shirt pocket where he had slipped the pictures. "Here's my lawyer's information. She'll set up payment. Whatever is easier for you."

She nodded, but her stomach turned. If he was paying child support, he'd start thinking he could have more say in Rosemarie's life. She wasn't ready to share her.

An awkward silence fell between them. When they had first met, talking had been so easy. They would stay on the beach late into the night discussing family, horses, the plans he had for the ranch, the boats he wanted to buy.

Sometimes they just talked about silly things that didn't matter. All that counted was that they were together. He was only two years older, but she had been eighteen. The world had revolved around him and he owned it all. She never could figure out what he had seen in that shy, clumsy girl.

Leaning on his elbows and lacing his fingers together, he stared straight at her. "I'm really trying to understand. I know I scared you, but how could you keep her from me for so long?"

The hard lines on his face and the white in his knuckles betrayed the anger he was holding in.

She shifted in her seat and looked away. It was hard to forget how strong her love for him had been in the early days. Then, a few months into their marriage, the drinking had started. That's what she needed to remember. "You had become too unpredictable."

"You didn't even give me a chance." His voice was low and harsh.

"I tried to help. When you had a difficult time with my parents or your uncle, I tried to intervene, but I know now that I only made it worse."

She had been so sheltered, and it had shocked her to see at firsthand how ugly people could be to the ones they loved. Elijah's uncle Frank had been a cruel, violent man who had no problem hitting someone small or weaker. The people he should have protected.

She shook her head. "I didn't have the life experience to help you. I couldn't imagine being abandoned by a mother and abused by an uncle. When it got worse, you started stumbling home hours after dinner. The one person I would have turned to for help was the one I was afraid for. I didn't know how to get you to stop drinking."

He grunted.

She knew Elijah had been suffering, but the more she had tried to help him, the worse the problems grew.

Looking down, she captured her hands and held them still. Her napkin was now an organized pile of neat shreds.

"The night I was going to tell you I was pregnant was the night you really seemed out of control. I thought about all the horror stories I'd heard about your uncle and the abuse. It overwhelmed me. I was scared of you." The cold seeped through her skin.

"I'm not my uncle." His voice was hard.

She wasn't sure if he was trying to convince her or himself.

If Elijah was truly sober, then she owed it to her daughter to let her know him. But it didn't mean she had to trust him.

He pulled out the pictures again.

With his attention on the photos, she had the luxury of studying him. His golden skin looked darker, but he had lighter streaks in his hair. The stubble from this afternoon was gone, leaving his skin smooth. Had he shaved for her?

With a heavy sigh, he looked up at the night sky. The string of white party lights highlighted his features. "I don't even know where to start. We had a baby. I still can't believe you left without telling me." Lowering his head, he stared straight at her.

Gripping the edge of the wooden seat, she forced herself to sit still. Despite the anger that radiated from him, his body language told her he was in control.

He had a right to be upset, but she couldn't back down. "The minute I found out I was pregnant, that baby became the most important person in my world." She allowed her brain to take her back to that night.

She would not regret her decision. "You were out of control. Each night was getting worse. I was waiting up later and later. When you finally came home, it was an hour of yelling and ranting before you passed out. The violence was escalating. That last night I was so scared."

"I never hurt you." His lips tightened as his hard jaw flexed. "Did I?"

He looked down, but not before she had seen anger mixed with loathing. And something else. Doubt?

She sat back. "Not physically."

"I'm not my uncle. I would never have touched you with violence." His voice was low and gravelly. "Why didn't you talk to me? Maybe if you had told me, I would've sobered up sooner."

Now her own anger burned. "Are you serious?" The words forced their way out from between clenched teeth. "I did talk. You had three modes." She held up one finger, keeping her scar facing her. "Drunk." The second finger went up. "Asleep." Then the third, the one she used to wear her wedding ring on. "Hungover. When was I supposed to reason with you?"

"You took my child and ran." He closed his eyes and rolled his shoulders. When he opened them, his gaze bored into her. He appeared calm, but clearly determined.

"When I spoke to my lawyer about child support, I also asked her to look into my rights as a father. I want to see my daughter. What does she know about me?"

Fear jumbled her insides into a big ball of mush. This was what she had been afraid of, the one thing she wanted to avoid at all costs. "I've never hidden you from her." Much to her mother's dismay. "I've shared a couple of pictures of us from when we were dating. She knows that her name is a combination of her father's family name and my grandmother's name."

"Why does she think I'm not around?" Tension reappeared in his shoulders. "Does she know you stole her?"

She leaned closer to him. "I did not kidnap my daughter." He needed to understand that her daughter, their daughter, was the most important person in this mess.

"I was protecting her the only way I knew how. You'd started drinking. I was not going to bring my baby into a house where objects went crashing into walls without warning or wait around to see if you got better." Over Elijah's shoulder, she saw the cheerful waitress heading to their table carrying a tray that held chips and guacamole, as well as a glass pitcher full of lemonade with fresh sliced lemons.

Twisting, he looked to see what had caused her to stop talking. With a tight smile, he thanked the blonde.

"Did you need menus, Mr. De La Rosa?"

He looked at Jazmine.

She shook her head. "No. I had dinner already." She wasn't even sure she could keep down the lemonade.

"We're good, Jenny. If I need anything else, I'll come in and let you know."

"Yes, sir." With one more perfect smile and a polite but curious look, she left.

Did Elijah bring dates here a lot?

That was none of her business.

It was back to the heavy silence. The discussion had derailed again. Years ago, she had put all the anger and bitterness behind her. Or at least she thought she had. "Elijah—"

"I want—"

Speaking on top of each other, they both stopped. His fingers ran over the surface of the envelope. Had she made a mistake?

The real question was, did she make it six years ago or tonight, like her mother thought?

He laced his fingers in front of him. With his head down like that, he looked as if he were praying. Maybe she should join him. The only thing she knew right now was that God had to be in control. Because she and Elijah had made a mess. She didn't want their daughter paying the price.

He cleared his throat. "Sorry. It's been a few years since I've had to go through this. I've forgotten how difficult it could be."

Confused, her gaze scanned his face, looking for clues to what he was thinking. He had always been good at hiding his feelings. "What do you mean?"

"Letting people air the hurts I caused them without getting defensive. It's part of the program, the twelve steps. The list I started telling you about at the mission, but we got a little distracted. I have to find each one and express my true regret for the damage I've done. The person I hurt gets to vent and I listen. No excuses,

I just listen. You were the only one left on my list. The last one. The one who deserves the biggest apology." He reached across the table like he wanted to touch her, but then pulled back.

"I destroyed our marriage with my drinking. I... I know I did that. Those are the words that I've wanted to say to you, and I mean every single one of them. You had every right to walk out, but we have a daughter now and I'm at a loss as to what that means. It's another horrible casualty of my drinking, but the thought of everything I missed is killing me. I can't get back those years."

"That's why I'm here. But I have to be honest. Trusting you again is not going to be easy. I'm worried."

He nodded, then looked up and made eye contact. "I'm sober. Soon it will be six years. I can't fix the past, but we can move forward. I want to see her tomorrow."

Chewing on the inside of her cheek, she organized her thoughts before answering. "You might have been sober for years, but in my mind, it was just the other day that you..." She looked down. "It might be best if we wait a little longer."

He tossed his head back and stared at the night sky again. His chest expanded with deep, hard breaths. "Maybe it would be better for everyone if we finish this discussion in a courtroom. I'll call my lawyer in the morning."

His full attention was back on her. The eyes that she used to stare into for hours now looked at her with anger. Not filled with the love from the beginning or the drunk haze they held last time she saw him, but clear crisp determination.

Her stomach turned. "Elijah, I don't—"

"I'm not the poor ranch kid from six years ago. If we have to go to court, I will. I deserve to have her in my life."

She held up her hand. "No."

He put his hands on top of hers, gently holding it to the table. Nerves tingled up her arm and down her spine. She stared at the hands that use to hold her with tenderness before the drinking. Clearing her head, she tried to pull away.

At first he increased the pressure, but then let her go.

"I won't—" His voice was low and calm, but she didn't doubt his iron will.

"Elijah, I didn't mean you can't see her. I just don't want to drag her through court. I came here tonight so we can work something out between us. Her parents."

Finally breaking eye contact, he propped his

elbows on the table and rested his forehead on his palms. "What about your parents? Every time I tried to get in contact with you, they had restraining orders thrown at me. What makes you think they'll go along with this now?"

Cutting her gaze to the busy restaurant, Jazmine felt thankful to be in public. It would help them both keep emotions in check.

"You know your drinking was very hard on them. That might be the one thing they can never forgive you for. You know our family history." She blinked back the wetness in her eyes.

With a tight nod, Elijah acknowledged the horrible truth. Her parents had lost a child because of a drunk driver. His gut burned. There was nothing to say to that.

"I'll take care of my parents. I came here tonight because it's time Rosemarie met her father. But Elijah, it has to be on my terms. I know there's a whole family she needs to meet, but please give me time. It's been just her and me. Bringing you into her life is not easy."

He wanted to point out that she had made this hard, not him. "I want to see her tomorrow."

"Okay, but not alone. That's my stipulation.

I can't trust you yet. Besides, she doesn't know you. To her, you're a stranger."

A sadness replaced the fury. "Because you took her from me." The words fought against the rawness in his throat.

She swallowed. "To protect her. She's very shy. If you come over for lunch, it will be a comfortable and safe way to introduce you."

"And she knows I'm her father, right?"

"In the abstract, which doesn't mean much to a five-year-old. I'll make sure she knows who you are."

He sat back. "Okay. Tomorrow at 11:30. Will that work?" Elijah dropped his gaze from his wife—his ex-wife.

She still hadn't said anything. This Jazmine was stronger. Surer of herself. But she couldn't keep his daughter from him. "Jazz? Eleven thirty tomorrow?"

She gave the slightest jerk of her head. "Elijah, you have to know this is hard for me. My last memories of you are… Well, they don't reassure my maternal fears. You've had years of being sober, but in my heart it all just happened."

The tension was back. "You really think I would hurt our child? That I would hurt any kid?" He wasn't that messed up.

Staying steady and calm was more important than his tattered pride. In the last five years, he had learned to listen and to wait before responding. It took time to process information and...ugh, feelings.

Even thinking the word to himself made him feel like an idiot. It was hard to completely erase his uncle's words from his mind. *Crybaby. Worthless. Weak. Waste of space.* How could a dead man still taunt him?

His uncle had spouted nothing but hatred and lies. He knew that now. But it was still hard not to get lost in the black hole of doubt that swirled in his brain whenever life hit him with an unexpected hailstorm.

In God's eyes, he was worthy of love. He was a child of God. That's what his sister, Belle, and his friend Miguel told him anyway, and if he was going to believe a lie, it was better to go with that one.

What did he know? One fact that was drilled into the smallest fiber of his being was that he would do whatever it took to have his daughter in his life. He didn't want to cause her any embarrassment or give her any reason not to claim him as her dad. *Dad.* He closed his eyes. He was someone's dad.

Daughter. Wow. He was prepared to face any of the consequences his drinking brought to his door, or so he thought. This, he had not seen coming. He opened his eyes and studied his ex-wife.

She was staring out over the water. She hadn't answered him, or he hadn't heard her.

"I wouldn't. You know that, right? I'd never hurt someone weaker than me."

"No. Not intentionally. But when you're drunk, your impulses and—"

"Which is why I don't drink anymore." Was he ever going to truly get away from his past? "Jazz, I know words aren't enough. Earning your trust is a task I'm up for. Let me show you."

Lips tight, she nodded. "That's why you're coming over. Rosemarie also needs time to get to know you." She looked at the sailboat outlined with cords of white patio lights, its reflection slowly dancing on the water as laughter floated through the air. Looking back at him, her eyes shimmered. "We'll see you tomorrow at 11:30."

Her face might have the grimmest expression, but he wanted to lift her up and swing her around. It had been a long time since he just wanted to laugh. She used to give him that. And then he had destroyed her light, pitching them both into darkness.

Now he had another opportunity. Lunch with his daughter was now on his agenda.

And just like that, the fear was back.

What if he messed this up? What if she didn't like him? He was a stranger to her. He twisted the leather at his wrist and repeated the words from his recent meditation verse, from John 14:27. He had needed an extra one today. *Let not your heart be troubled, neither let it be afraid.*

He needed to let the fear move on, through and out.

She stood, seemingly unaware of the turbulent sea of his emotions. "Now that we have that settled, I need to go home. I'll see you tomorrow. Mom will have Daddy at PT, so it will just be the three of us."

Pushing back the chair, he got to his feet and pulled out his business card. As he held it out, his work-hardened hands grazed her soft skin. The instinct to put her hand to his lips had to be locked down tight. "My personal cell is written on the back. If you don't want to go through my lawyer, let me know whatever you need."

"Thanks."

He wanted to keep her here longer, but couldn't think of any way to do it without kidnapping her. That wouldn't help with the trust issues. "I'll see y'all tomorrow. Do I need to bring anything?"

She swung the strap of her purse over her shoulder. "Just yourself."

He wanted to ask her if he would be enough, but he stopped himself. Did he really want to know the truth?

As they walked to the exit, the singer started to cover "Just the Way You Are." Jazmine jerked her head up to his, her eyes wide. "Did you—"

"No." The words to their song swirled around him. "Just a coincidence." Possibly a very cruel one. The memory of holding her while they slow-danced flooded his mind, and his body didn't seem to notice the time difference. He was there with her. Back when she still loved him. More importantly, she had trusted him.

Lips tight, she turned from him. "Bye. We'll see you tomorrow."

His eyes followed her until she vanished from his sight. He needed to take some sort of gift. There wasn't a thing about him that would make an impression on a five, almost six-year-old girl. *His* five, almost six-year-old girl. What did little girls like?

Pulling his phone out, he called his sister. It was time to let his family know. Belle was obsessive about family sticking together. He wasn't sure if she was going to be more upset with him or with Jazmine and her parents. Either way he was in for a lecture about family.

Chapter Four

Elijah slowly pulled his truck into the brick driveway. The looming, three-story beach house with its wraparound porches and floor-to-ceiling windows always made him feel as if he didn't measure up.

Jazmine had laughed and said it was just a house. But that's what she didn't get. To her, it was just an ordinary vacation house. In his world, even the idea of a vacation house was extraordinary, let alone the design and size of this one.

His family had a ranch along the coast that included waterfront property, but they were considered land-poor at best. What was the point of owning land worth millions if you struggled to pay your basic living expenses?

Parking in front of the huge garage door that looked as though it belonged on an English carriage house, he tilted his head to look up. They had spent so much time sitting on the top balcony, staring at the stars, listening to the water. Those had been the best days of his life. Back when she had drowned out his uncle's voice.

Of course, when her parents found them one night, they had been fit to be tied. They didn't care that the most he and Jazmine had ever done was hold hands. In their mind, he was a De La Rosa and would contaminate their daughter. He hated himself for proving them right. This morning's devotional ran through his head again. *Don't be anxious. Stay in prayer.*

Easier said than done. His skin itched. Not the kind of itch that you could scratch, but under his skin. It was the kind that reminded him that he was an alcoholic, and that the minute he forgot it he would be in big trouble.

Stepping out of the truck, he centered himself before opening the door to the backseat. He hoped he hadn't gotten the gift wrong. A movement on the top balcony caught his attention. A mini Jazmine was looking over the railing. Her thick, dark, corkscrew curls framed her tiny golden-brown face.

All the blood left his body. When he'd seen her the first time, he hadn't known who she was. His brain hadn't had time to process that she was real. A little person that was part of him and Jazmine. He wanted to stare at her, take the time to make sure every detail was branded in his memory. But he needed to move, do something. He waved. "Hi, Rose-marie." His voice cracked. *Really?*

He was an idiot. *Great first impression, De La Rosa.*

She darted away. "Momma! He's here!"

A few seconds later, mother and daughter were looking down at him. Something he couldn't identify pushed at his insides.

"Hey," he called up to them. "Should I climb up the side like the old days?" There was elaborate ironwork decorating the side of the house.

"Elijah De La Rosa, don't you dare."

Rosemarie studied him wide-eyed, then turned to her mother. "He can climb the wall like Spider-Man?"

He grinned. "Sure. I used to do it all the time."

"No. You stay right there. We're coming down to let you in."

He chuckled. Getting her riled had been one of his favorite things to do. Probably not a good idea now. By the time she opened the door, he was requesting wisdom and strength from God again.

Jazmine stepped back to let him enter the downstairs foyer. This was the plainest part of the house. It was designed to take water during heavy storms. The main living area was on the second floor and the bedrooms on the third.

With a hesitant move, Jazmine turned to the stairs.

His heart hit harder with each step, steps that brought him to his daughter. Most fathers had nine months to get used to the idea of having a child. A tiny wiggling infant was placed in their arms, and each month their baby grew into more of a little person.

Jazmine stopped on the last step. He was behind her but didn't see his daughter. His gaze darted to Jazz. She gave him a half smile. Had his daughter already decide she didn't want to meet him?

"She's very shy." She glanced toward the upper level. "Rosemarie? Come on down, sweetheart."

The worn leather of his bracelet was warm between his thumb and finger. He had already seen her, so why was he so nervous now? They would be in the same room.

He kept his focus on the top of the stairs. If his heart beat any harder, it might break his ribs. Licking his lips, he discovered they were dry. Then that sweet face surrounded by dark curls peeked around the corner of the wall.

There were people in his life he loved, but at this moment he was hit hard by a love so wild and raw that his knees almost gave out.

"Hi, there. Rosemarie, right?" His eyes burned. *No, no, no.* He took a deep breath and unlocked his jaw. The last thing he wanted to do was to scare her.

She nodded, moving toward her mother one slow, agonizing step at a time. She eyed him as if he was a coiled rattlesnake. Her hand stayed on the railing. The wall behind her was covered with photos. Rosemarie's pictures hung with the other members of the Daniels family, including the boy they had lost.

Jazmine had said she didn't have many memories of her older brother. He had been killed when she was only three. Sweat broke out across Elijah's body.

The family had to hate that their only surviving child had married an alcoholic. He had a lot to prove, but first he wanted to see his daughter smile. He lowered himself to a crouch, so he wouldn't tower over her.

Finally, she made it to her mother's side, and wrapped an arm around Jazmine's jean-clad leg.

"Hi, Rosemarie." He tried again, making sure to give her an easy smile. "I'm..." *Your dad, father, daddy.* Each word clogged his throat. None of them sounded right. "I'm so happy to meet you."

"You're my daddy, right?" Her tiny, bow-shaped lips twisted to the side.

He couldn't breathe for a minute. "I am."

"Momma calls Papa Daddy. Is that what I should call you?"

Everything below his neck locked up. He managed a nod and what he hoped was an encouraging smile. "If you want to. I like it."

Silence slipped between them again. What topics of conversation did a father have with a five-year-old daughter he'd never met?

Jazmine ran her hands over their daughter's head, pushing back her hair. "I think he has a gift for you." She raised her eyebrows and looked pointedly at the bag in his right hand.

"Oh. Yeah." He lifted the bright pink bag. "I brought this for you. My sister helped me pick it out. You can call her Tía Belle or Aunt Belle. She has a little girl about your age. You have a few cousins and a couple of aunts." Great, now he was babbling. He tried to laugh, but it sounded more like a cat caught in a trap. "Want to know a secret?"

She nodded but didn't step away from her mother.

"I'm a bit nervous." He leaned closer, stopping himself from reaching out to touch her.

Nodding to the bag, he offered it to her again. "I hope you like it. If you don't, we can trade it in for something else."

Taking the bag, she smiled at him. He didn't know it was possible for a heart to hold a beat.

Rosemarie peered into the colorful wrapping his sister had chosen for him and gasped. He wanted to know if it was a good or bad noise.

"Momma, look! I'm naming her Zoe! She and Abby'll be best friends." She pulled out the dark-haired doll and hugged her. "Thank you." Turning to her mother, she held up the doll. "Can I take her to lunch?"

"That's a wonderful idea." Jazmine looked at Elijah. "She set her table for us. She wanted all her friends to meet you."

"Friends?" His gut tightened. "I thought…" Narrowing his eyes, he studied Jazmine. Her dark eyes gleamed like they used to whenever she messed with him.

"Yes!" Rosemarie interrupted his thoughts. "Mary has somewhere very important to go, so Zoe can have her spot." The little girl nodded somberly before skipping through the kitchen to the back door. Through the large glass panels, Elijah could see the ocean.

"Come." Jazmine followed her daughter. "She might not seem excited that you're here, but she set the table and helped my mother make fresh lemonade. I told her how we used to drink it during the summer while we sat on the pier and watched the waves. She planned the menu."

"You told her about us?"

"The good parts."

Swallowing the bitterness, he inhaled. He couldn't remember the last time he'd had to use his calming strategies so often in one day. "Your mother helped her? Will it be safe for me to eat?"

One hand on the door, Jazmine paused. For a moment she studied his face with a fierce intensity. Was she going to kick him out?

He held his breath as he waited for the verdict. "Sorry." He made a note to lay off the mother jokes.

"She's a little girl. A little girl who lives in a world where everybody loves her and cares for her. Please don't be her first heartbreak."

The first instinct was to deny he would ever do anything to hurt her, but then he stopped. He had blown his promises to honor and protect Jazmine out of the water. He had broken her heart.

Rubbing the back of his neck, he glanced to the little girl. She was talking to a line of stuffed animals and dolls. "I'm in a different place now. I don't know how to promise never to hurt her, but I'm going to do my best."

Their gazes stayed locked for longer than he could count.

He must have passed her test because she nodded, then crossed the threshold. To the far right, in the shaded area on the large balcony, was a mini pink picnic table. There were purple and green chairs at each end. They were a bit higher than the yellow benches on either side, but not by much.

Starfish, seashells and driftwood decorated the center, and pretty teacups and delicate plates were set at each place. The doll he had given her was in the middle of a militant line of other dolls and animals. She came over and took his hand.

"This is your spot." There was a pause. "Daddy." She stood next to the plastic chair at the end of the table. One brow up, he eyed the little polka-dot piece of furniture. Serious doubts flooded his brain.

With a huge smile, Jazmine took the chair opposite. Slowly, he followed suit, easing himself down onto the fragile frame. His knees came halfway to his chest.

"So, these lovely ladies are your friends?"

"Yes." She went on to introduce him to each

one, then picked up a small pitcher with both hands. "May I pour a drink for you?"

"I would love that. Thank you." He wanted to reach out and help her as wobbly hands tipped the pitcher, but he held back. He recognized that determined expression.

Her tongue stuck out at the corner of her mouth as she concentrated, and he felt his own mouth twitch. She looked just like his sister when she was focused on a task.

Rosemarie moved down the side of the table and poured a little in each small cup. As she served her posse, she told him how she had met each one.

No surprise that his daughter had a very vivid imagination. He had loved reading and making up stories. His sister and cousins had been participants in many of his imaginary adventures. Uncle Frank had called him a lazy dreamer.

The doll he had given her sat next to a royally dressed Abby. Apparently, she was the queen of all the other toys.

There was a bowl of chips and salsa on the table. Rosemarie offered him a small plate. "Would you like some appetizer?"

It took him a minute to figure out what she was saying. "Chips are my favorite."

He glanced at Jazmine, and she flashed him

a proud smile. It was a good look. She wasn't his Jazz anymore. In the last six years she had grown up, became a mother.

Rosemarie finished serving everyone, then tucked her sundress under her as she sat. Just like a little lady. "For lunch we're eating flautas. Momma told me how you taught her how to make them when you didn't have enough money. She said you ate them all the time."

He frowned at Jazz. She had told their daughter he hadn't had enough money to feed them?

He smiled at Rosemarie. "I'm impressed you did your research." Elijah was pretty sure he had never eaten with a party of stuffed toys before. Not sure how to start a conversation, he took a slow sip of lemonade.

His daughter reached over to feed a doll, then looked at him. "Abby would like to know if you still have horses. She has a pony, but we had to leave it back home. Prince is a pretty palomino."

Before he said anything, a timer went off. Rosemarie popped up. "That's the flautas."

Jazmine got up from her chair.

"No, Momma. Stay here and talk with Daddy. I can get them."

Instead of sitting as her daughter told her to, Jazmine shook her head. "Rosemarie Daniels!"

"Momma, I'm a big girl. I want to make lunch. I don't need help." She pouted.

"You can't open the oven by yourself, young lady. It's dangerous."

With a sigh bigger than her small shoulders, Rosemarie followed her mother into the house. Elijah sat alone.

Well, not completely alone. All the little dolls glared at him. He looked down, breaking eye contact with the toys, and stared at his intertwined fingers.

Daniels. It tore at his gut that his daughter didn't have his name. How did he fix this? His relationship with Jazmine might be beyond repair, but he had a second chance with his daughter.

His ex-wife and her parents were going to have to deal with the fact that Rosemarie had another parent who loved her too. There would be no doubt in his daughter's mind that she was loved by her father. She wouldn't grow up with his issues.

Now he just had to show Jazmine that he could be trusted with their daughter's heart. She had every reason in the world to doubt him.

Lifting his head, he found the dolls staring silently at him, judging him.

"Yes, I know," he whispered to the toys. On their wedding day he had promised to cherish and honor her. But in grand De La Rosa fashion, he had broken her.

The downstairs door opened and closed. Glancing at the clock, Jazmine frowned. It was too early for her parents to be back. Her mother had agreed to stay away for two hours. Slipping the round stone onto the cooling rack, she helped Rosemarie move the tightly rolled corn tortillas filled with refried beans onto a serving plate.

Rosemarie looked up at her and smiled. "Papa and GiGi are here! They can meet my father and eat lunch with us." Like a good little hostess, her expression changed to panic. "Do we have enough?"

"We're good. Take this out to your father." *Wow.* Words she wasn't using to saying. "I'll be right there."

What was her parents doing here? Jazmine snorted as her irritation grew.

There had been very loud complaints about her and Rosemarie meeting with Elijah alone. Her mother had wanted to be here, but Jazmine had insisted she could handle the meeting alone.

She glanced out the kitchen window to

make sure Rosemarie was safe. Her heart still bounced at the thought of Elijah being with her daughter. She needed to start thinking of her as *their* daughter.

Rosemarie laughed. The sound was all joy, free of adult angst.

He was going to be a part of her life now. She sighed. Azalea would have to learn how to deal with it.

Elijah's broad back was to her, so she couldn't see his expression, but he was sitting at the kiddie table as though he did this all the time. When Rosemarie had first asked to serve lunch on her little table, Jazmine had liked the thought of making Elijah uncomfortable. To test him, see if he was ready to be a real father to a little girl.

Part of her would have been happy if he hadn't shown up.

"Did you leave her out there alone with him?" Her mother's voice was at its coldest setting.

"I had planned to be out there, but someone didn't stick to the plan." Jazmine twisted the corner of her mouth as she glared at her mother. Then she realized her father wasn't with them.

Her heart plunged. "Is something wrong with Daddy?"

With pursed lips, her mother shook her head. She started removing her stylish blazer. "He's good. His friend Larry is with him, and they wanted to sit by the pool and visit. Larry will help him up the stairs in just a bit. Two hours is too long for him to be out. It was the perfect time to touch base and see how it was going."

Craning her neck to look out the window, she made a disgruntled noise. "It's a bad idea to have him here alone with you. He's an acholic."

"Mother, it's the middle of the day, and I wouldn't have let him in if he had been drinking." She picked up the purse her mother had placed on the counter and handed it to her. "Go. I told him it would just be the three of us for two hours. It hasn't even been thirty minutes yet. Don't turn me into a liar. They need a chance to get to know each other."

"He lost that chance when he picked up a bottle." Ignoring the elegant leather bag, Azalea walked past her toward the outside door.

Jazmine rushed to cut her mother off. "Rosemarie has a father, and we are going to learn to deal with that. Please go back to Daddy. I've got this."

A scream came from the balcony. Both women lunged for the door.

Chapter Five

Jazmine stopped when she saw Rosemarie jump up and down, then throw herself at Elijah. The force of her energy unbalanced his chair, throwing him backward. With one hand he caught himself and braced Rosemarie with the other.

Azalea was over him in a flash. She scooped up Rosemarie, pulling the little girl against her as if saving her from certain death.

"What's wrong, baby girl?" she fussed.

Elijah jumped to his feet and dusted off his pants. He gave Jazmine a guilty look.

She narrowed her eyes at him. "What happened?"

His gray-green eyes darted from her to the Gulf. "I kinda of...um. We were—"

"He's giving me a horse of my very own!"

"What!" Both women turned to him, eyes wide.

"You promised her a horse?" Azalea glared at him. "How irresponsible are you? You never grew up, did you? You're the same—"

"Mother. Stop." Jazmine turned to Elijah. "You promised her a horse?"

"A real one, Momma. He said I can pick it out. I want a palomino." Rosemarie craned back to look at her grandmother. "And he's a pirate. My dad is a real pirate."

"I'm not a—"

As one, the mother and daughter team turned their glares to him again. The displeasure on Azalea's face was tangible. "You told her you're a pirate?"

"He owns a pirate ship." Turning from her grandmother, Rosemarie faced her father. "Right, Daddy? And fishing boats." With a huge grin, she touched her grandmother's face. "We can go fishing, and he said we could go to his ranch and pick out a horse."

"His ranch?" Sarcasm dripped like honey from Azalea's lips.

Jazmine cut her mother off before the insults started flying again. "Mother, could you take Rosemarie into the kitchen? Maybe eat one of the brownies we made."

"But we haven't finished lunch, and I made the brownies for Daddy!"

Jazmine's eyes started burning. She hadn't

thought her daughter would bond this quickly to Elijah. Of course, she didn't know that he would give her a horse or tell her five-year-old he was a pirate. Between gritted teeth, she forced a smile. "Go with GiGi."

The small shoulders slumped. "Can I take Zoe?" The voice that had been so happy just a bit ago was now trembling. Big tears were building in those sweet eyes as she looked up at her father. "I made brownies for you."

Elijah stepped closer, then dropped down to one knee. "It's okay. I'm not leaving without saying goodbye." He picked up the doll and handed it to her. "Go with your grandmother."

It grated on Jazmine's nerves that he stepped in and acted like a parent. Closing her eyes, she took a deep breath. "He's not going anywhere, sweetheart. We'll be inside to have a brownie in a moment."

Her mother scoffed and turned away. She was not making this easier.

"Mother, be nice." She leaned in closer. "Please, keep your personal opinions to yourself."

Once they were alone, Elijah righted the chair. "Listen. I'm—"

"No. This is not the kind of thing you can just say 'Oops, my bad' and then go on your merry way. You can't make that kind of promise. And why are you lying to her about being a pirate?"

Tilting her head back, she looked to the sky for answers. *God, please help me here.* "Elijah, you don't have to impress her." She came back to his guilty face. "You're her father. She automatically loves you until you break her heart. Don't lie to her."

"I'm not lying. I do own a pirate ship." He stuffed his hands into his pressed jeans. "I don't captain it, so I don't think I can claim piratehood. I didn't tell her I was a pirate. I offered to take her out on the water. It's fun. The crew dresses up. Pretending to be a free and reckless pirate is a safe way to create an adventure. I told her she could be the brave daughter of a pirate. But no stealing. We don't steal." He winked at her, trying to lighten the mood, but his smile was sad.

He had stolen. He had taken her dreams, her heart. Falling in love with the bad-boy pirate had been exciting and fun. Each day had been a new adventure with him. It had been the greatest time of her life.

The last few months of their marriage? Not so much.

"I have a whole fleet. I'm living the life we used to dream about. Remember all those crazy plans for owning boats and running the ranch?" One hip propped against the railing, he crossed his arms over his chest and stared out over the water. "After I got sober, I made my dream of being a pirate cowboy come true. Crazy, right?"

She didn't even know how to respond to that. "You." She pointed at him. "You own a pirate ship?" Her mouth dropped open as she thought back to last night. "The restaurant? How?"

He took a deep breath as though he was going to confess a deep, dark secret and nodded. "I told you I wasn't a poor ranch kid anymore. You know how they say the storms of our lives can be blessings in disguise?" His Spanish-moss eyes burned with intensity, waiting for something.

She nodded, not sure what else to do. Elijah had never been a liar, not until he started hiding his drinking.

He shifted and braced his hand on the railing. "I lost my office job the Monday after you left. No one would take my calls."

She would not feel sorry for him. She wouldn't.

"My uncle was not an option. I went to the pier and took any job they'd give me. Working the recreational fishing boats, I met Miguel Valencia. We had an opportunity to buy a charter fishing boat, and he became my business partner. I always loved working outdoors meeting different people. I found my place." The smile on his lips contrasted with the sadness in his eyes.

"That sounds like a perfect career choice for you." He had hated working in an office. Even if it had been one of the nicest offices in the county.

On the water behind them, a boat was making its way to the bay. "We bought one boat that had been damaged in the storm and fixed it up. We put all our profits into the business. It grew." He pointed to the boat full of people. "That's one of ours. Now we have four fishing boats and a sightseeing boat. We opened the Painted Dolphin and just added the pirate ship. There are several other threads to our business, and now that my uncle is dead, I'm working with my sister and cousins to expand the income for the ranch. We might sell it, not sure yet. We're looking at hosting a fishing tournament and rodeo event as a huge community festival. We need to start small but… well, we tend to expand quickly."

"You own your own businesses and are developing community events?" This was so hard to compute. Yesterday morning she had thought he was homeless, only to find out he owned half the businesses on the waterfront.

Her parents had to have known, but they hadn't said a word to her. "The Painted Dolphin is yours?" Her brain was having a problem re-calibrating.

"Yep. We bought the pier. We're restoring a bit at a time. We have more than sixty people working for us now. The summer numbers are higher because of tourism." He turned away from the beach view and focused on her. "I talked to my lawyer this morning."

Her stomach clenched. He had the resources to take her to court. She had basically stolen his child.

He studied her. "She has the amount I owe for the past five—"

"No. I don't need your money. That's not why I came back."

"When she's older, I want her to know I was responsible. I also want to be a part of her life. On all levels. You had to know I would have strong feelings about supporting my daughter. Don't fight me on this." His lips formed a hard line. "I want to take care of her."

Nodding, she stepped back, away from the familiar scent that made her want to curl into him.

When they had been together, one of his fa-vorite things to do had been to lean in close to her ear with one hand in her hair and the other on the center of her back. He'd hold her against him and whisper that he'd take care of her, like the princess she was.

Unfortunately, she had believed him until it had been too late. He hadn't even been able to take care of himself. Over the last five years, though, she had stepped out of her parent's shadow and stood on her own. She'd raised their daughter.

She bit at her lip. Back in the beginning, she imagined they were taking care of each other, but she couldn't really say that, either. She hadn't been strong enough to take on his struggle, to break the chains that held him to the past.

He had been fighting a fight she couldn't win for him.

Moving to face the Gulf, Elijah braced his hands on the top of the railing. "Jazz, I'm sorry about the horse. But I meant it. We can go out to the ranch. We have a stable of very well-behaved horses that we use for beach rides."

"That's not the issue. You could have a hundred horses. We live in an apartment in Denver. We don't have the space or time for a horse. I'm her mother. You can't just start making promises without talking to me. That's basic parenting."

"When she started talking about how much

she loved horses and had always wanted one, I got excited I could give her that. That's something I can do. My businesses are doing well." He paused. "I want to take care of you the way I should have for the last six years."

"You and I are over. All she needs is a father who will be there for her."

With a sigh, she glanced into the kitchen. Rosemarie was waving her hands around as she told her GiGi some grand story. "Now I'm the one who has to tell her 'No.' Don't make any more promises to her without talking to me first. Okay?"

He twisted his lips and squinted one eye.

That wasn't good. "What is it, Elijah? Just spit it out."

"I, um…asked her about her birthday. As we were talking about that, I kind of told her we could have a big birthday party on the pirate ship. That's how we got to talking about birthday wishes. She told me that every year of her life she wished for a pony and never got one. So, I—"

Jazmine couldn't help the chuckle that escaped. "No. No pirate ships. She's going to be six. So, her whole life thing is a bit dramatic. She loves theatrical statements. You should have seen the fits she could throw for the first three years. I'm happy to report the tantrums have been a thing of the past since she turned four."

He grinned. "You were never dramatic. Always even-keeled, the practical girl. The drama sounds more like my sister."

Tired, Jazmine sat. She rolled her head back, looking up at the clear sky. "Yeah, I remember that. My parents like to blame any hint of a bad character flaw on your family."

"Of course, they would. Unfortunately, they're probably right. I'm sure she takes after you more than me." He eased down on the chair next to her. "Speaking of my sister, Belle wants her to meet her daughters, Cassie and Lucy. Lucy is Rosemarie's age."

"I remember when Cassandra was born. Belle and Jared run the ranch?"

His mouth tightened. "They split up during her last pregnancy. Right after you left. She'd been running the ranch on her own for Uncle Frank."

"What about Xavier and Damian? You were always close to your cousins."

With a deep sigh, he rubbed his forehead. "Damian came back from a tour in Afghanistan. He's not doing too well. He's pretty much isolated himself in the back forty on the ranch." He paused, his mouth tight.

"Xavier." His jaw set, he took a deep inhale

through his nose. "He returned from the Middle East, but then he took a security job down in Colombia. He didn't make it back. His team was ambushed. None of them made it out."

She sat up and grabbed his hand. "Oh Elijah. I'm so sorry. I know how close you were to him. Poor Selena. They were together since middle school. Do they have kids?"

"She found out she was pregnant, and a month later we got word that he was killed." His throat sounded rough. "He never knew they were expecting."

She studied his face, but didn't see anything but a clear expression, devoid of emotion. "I'm so sorry. That must be so hard."

"It was the closest I've come to ending my streak of sobriety." He looked at his hands before taking his gaze back to the Gulf. "Selena has triplets."

"Wow." She didn't know anyone who had triplets. "Are they here in town?"

"Yeah. I love playing uncle. But it's hard. They haven't started asking questions. They're too little. Xavier believed in me when I decided to fight to stay sober. He's—was—part owner of the business. If he was here he wouldn't allow me anywhere around his babies if I started drinking again."

Picking up one of the dolls, he fixed its little hat. "I'm sorry about the horse. I'll talk to her. And the birthday party. Tell her it was all my fault."

"By her birthday we should be back in Denver."

The silence fell with a heavy thud. All the unspoken words they were afraid to release swirled around them.

She finally stood. "Rosemarie is very excited about serving the brownies she made for you."

"You're the one who loved brownies." His features softened. "The gooey center."

The sweet memory warmed her. "You taught me to go for the center. I didn't have to wait until the edge was eaten." She wrapped her arms around her waist and studied her daughter through the window. "I told her how you would bring me warm brownies you made yourself. You'd cut the edges off and give them to me on Monday, so I'd have them all week."

Watching a pelican dive into the Gulf, he braced his arms on the railing. "Did you tell her it was because I didn't have money for flowers or fancy dinners?"

"Elijah, it was never about money for me. You taught me that it's the little things in life that bring the most joy." She closed her eyes and swallowed. The burn in her throat could not be allowed to rise. She would not cry for everything lost. "I've worked hard to pass that lesson on to her, so stop the over-the-top gestures."

Before he could respond, she hurried to the door. "Rosie's waiting." As she opened the door, his hand stopped her. For a second she wanted to lean into his warmth, but she made herself step back, pulling her arm out of his grasp.

Distance. It was important that she kept distance between them. She couldn't afford any closeness, physical, mental or spiritual. Talking about his family had been a mistake. They had all been so close at one time. She turned her back to him.

His fingers gave a gentle squeeze. "Jazz, can I join y'all? For her birthday. I'll fly to Denver if you're back there."

Closing her eyes, she managed a shrug. "We'll see." She was his daughter. Opening her eyes, she faced him. Avoiding him would not make this better. "Do me a favor and don't say anything yet. I'll talk to Mom. I'm sure we can work something out."

He snorted, letting her know what he thought of that. If Azalea had her way, he'd never be a part of Rosemarie's life.

If she thought he would go away as easily as

last time, she'd be in for a surprise. He wasn't the insecure poor ranch kid anymore, and now he had a daughter to fight for.

Chapter Six

Elijah watched Jazmine enter the house. Had he really thought the Daniels would allow him to meet Jazmine and Rosemarie without interference? Anger flared up, but he knew expressing it wouldn't do any good, no matter how righteous.

Mrs. Daniels smiled at Jazmine. "Larry settled your dad in the family room. I need to make sure he is in bed after his outing. This is not a good time for visitors."

"Mom, you agreed to give us two hours."

Arms around Rosemarie, Azalea glanced at Elijah, then moved on, like he wasn't even worth her time. She had made it clear he was not welcome. "This is our home. Your father needs rest."

Choices he made had created this mess, so he was just going to have to suck it up and smile.

Given time they would trust him. He'd been sober for five years now, but Jazz had reminded him that to them it was just yesterday.

He gave her his best smile. Being nice to difficult people was a gift that worked well for him in business, and he would use it now. There would be no pride getting in his way. His daughter was worth it.

"Mrs. Daniels, it's a pleasure. Thank you for letting me in your house."

"Daddy." Rosemarie jumped from the bar stool she sat on and darted over to a credenza. "Look!" She pulled out a realistic toy horse. "I want a horse just like Misty."

It was a prancing golden palomino with pink ribbon woven through the flaxen mane and tail. "That's a pretty pony. I might—"

Mrs. Daniels made a great show of clearing her throat. He sighed. Looking at the women, he knew he was on shaky ground.

She moved to stand in front of Rosemarie. Going down to eye level, she placed one hand on the small shoulder and gently took the horse with the other. "We've talked about this. Your mother doesn't have the room or time for a real horse. They need a great deal of care, and you haven't even had a dog yet."

"Mother." Jazmine's voice sounded tired or resigned. "I've already said no to a dog." She glanced at Elijah with a frown. He needed to be careful and not mess this up. There was so much he didn't know.

Tears started welling up in the little girl's big eyes. How did anyone say "No" to that? He sat on a chair next to his daughter and her grandmother. "We have dogs at the ranch. My sister's Australian shepherd had puppies. You could visit and play with them."

"Really?" The joy was back. Turning from her grandmother, she hugged him. He brought his hands around the tiny body. Her hair smelled like oranges. Closing his eyes, he made sure to take in everything about this moment.

He'd do anything for this little being that was a part of him and Jazmine.

She stepped back. The huge smile and sparkling eyes were about the sweetest thing he'd ever seen. He glanced up to Jazmine.

There was no sparkle there, and her full lips were thinned by tension.

"An Australian shepherd? Are they aggressive?" His ex-mother-in-law crossed her arms.

"They're one of the best breeds around kids." He leaned forward. "A couple of years ago when my niece was about three, she had figured out that she could open the door if she used a chair. Belle, my sister, was working in the kitchen and had no clue that Lucy had escaped the house."

Both women gasped.

"Frog followed her out and barked until my sister came." He chuckled. "Belle said it was the craziest thing to see. Little Lucy was trying her best to get to the barn. She wanted to go riding. Frog kept herding her back, cutting her off every time she tried to go through the yard gate. She didn't stop barking until she saw Belle."

He patted Rosemarie's shoulder. "So, once you belong to a shepherd, they're yours for life. She is the mother of the new pups."

"I want one. I want one of Frog's puppies."

Mrs. Daniels frowned. If looks had energy, he'd be burned to a crisp. She looked at her daughter, silently telling her to do something about this interloper. Elijah rested his elbow on the glass tabletop. He stared straight at her, making sure she understood that he was not going anywhere.

Jazmine sighed. "This will be a family discussion tonight after dinner. Okay?"

"But Momma, I want a dog. If I can't have a horse, can I get a dog?"

Jazz gave him a look that promised they would be talking later and he might not enjoy the conversation. He doubted there would be any conversation going on, more like a full-on lecture. He wanted to defend himself and point out he had not offered to give her a dog, just the time to play with one.

A kettle started whistling. Mrs. Daniels went to the stove top and poured the hot water into a tall thermal mug. "Come here, sweetheart, your papa needs his green tea."

Tucking her horse under her arm, Rosemarie skipped to her grandmother. "Yes, ma'am."

"You also need to give him his afternoon healing kiss." After putting the lid on the silver cup, she handed it to her granddaughter.

Rosemarie carefully carried the tea with both hands and disappeared into the front family room.

Elijah checked his watch. "It looks like a good time for me to leave." He spoke directly to Jazmine, making a point to ignore Azalea Daniels. "Maybe we can pick a neutral place tomorrow."

Jazmine's mother stared straight at him. "I'm not sure there is a place for you in Rosemarie's life."

"Mother." Jazmine's voice had a new edge.

He shook his head. "It's okay, Jazmine."

Turning to Azalea, he held eye contact. "I hurt your daughter. I get it. But I'm not the man I was."

He needed to be up front and clear. "I know firsthand what it's like to grow up without a father. Thank you for taking care of my daughter when I couldn't. But I'm here. I'm sober and I'm not going anywhere. I know it'll take time to build trust. But I will."

Azalea's mouth went tighter. She didn't believe a word he said, but that was fine.

"The people in my life who didn't believe in me have outnumbered the ones who did. I proved them wrong, and I'll do the same with you."

He turned to his ex-wife. Right now, she was the only one who mattered. Her parents had interfered with their marriage, and he had used drinking to hide from the problems instead of dealing with them head-on. This time had to be different. He was a father, and he had to be strong enough to claim that right.

Jazz was guiding his relationship with his daughter, and he wasn't going to let his past insecurities stop him from being the kind of father his daughter deserved. "I'll go for now." He hoped he looked a lot calmer than he felt. "Call me so we can make arrangements."

"Okay." Jazmine rubbed her head. She knew that her mother was only trying to help, but she was making it worse.

A crash from the family room shattered the tense silence. It was followed by her father yelling. Rosemarie ran to the door looking scared. "Papa fell."

Azalea rushed out of the kitchen. Jazmine stopped at the door and hugged her frightened daughter. Elijah stood right behind her.

"It'll be okay, baby." She took the small hand into hers.

Next to the hospital bed, her father lay on the floor, his tea running across the tile. He was pushing her mother away.

"I'm not an invalid, Lea. I can get up," he snarled at his wife.

Azalea ignored him. She had her hands under his arms, trying to lift him off the floor. "You almost died. You banged up your whole body, and you broke a couple of bones. So yes, for now you are an invalid. Deal with it. Where's Larry?"

"Woman, I can walk myself into the house." In the process of trying to free himself, he caused her mother to lose her balance, and she ended up on the floor beside him.

"Ugh. Stubborn man. What is your problem?" She sat up, shaking the liquid off her hands. "At this rate you're going to end up back in the hospital. Is that what you want?" She slipped off her heels, then stood over him with her hands on her hips, watching him as he struggled to sit up.

He leaned against the bed, looking defeated.

"Daddy, what are you doing? You scared Rosemarie. Why didn't you call for help and wait for one of us?" Going to the cabinet, Jazmine pulled out a roll of paper towels and cleaned up the mess. Her mother straightened the rumpled blankets. Elijah remained next to Rosie, his hand on her shoulder.

"I just wanted to watch the fishing show sitting in a chair. Is it too much to want to sit in a chair? I should be able to walk across the room and sit in a stupid chair."

"The doctor said that rest is the most important thing you could do. Do you want to die?"

"If I can't even sit in a chair? Maybe," he grumbled.

Her mother gasped. "Nelson James Daniels. Don't you say that!" Tears hovered on the edge of Azalea's dark eyes.

Rosemarie stepped away from Elijah. "Papa, why do you want to die?"

"Oh, no, sweetheart." He held his hand out to his granddaughter. "I'm just being a grumpy old man."

Elijah followed her and crouched so that he was shoulder to shoulder with Rosemarie. "I don't think the issue is sitting in the chair, but you might need to let them help you get to the chair."

Azalea took Rosemarie's hand and led her to the living room door. "Elijah, this is a family matter. You were leaving."

Rosemarie shook her head. "Not yet. Please don't go."

He glanced at Jazz, then her. He didn't say anything, waiting for them. Azalea sighed. "We'll go make you some more green tea. Maybe your papa will find his way into the bed where he should be resting." She lowered her chin and stared at her husband. "I guess you could do that in the chair just as well. When we get back, I expect you to be in the chair, so you can have tea with your granddaughter. Then you can say goodbye to…your father." Back straight, barefooted, she left the room.

After cleaning up the spilled tea, Jazmine went to the small sink that sat in the wood bar and made herself busy. He needed privacy and space to recover his pride, then she would offer to help him up before her mother returned.

She grunted. At this rate, if her mom didn't let up, her parents were going to kill each other.

From the corner of her eye she noticed Elijah sit on the floor next to her father. She turned to intervene. This was the last thing her father needed. He glared at the wall across the room, his eyes hard and cold. Elijah's voice was so low she couldn't hear him.

She moved closer, not sure if it was her father or her ex-husband she needed to protect. Before she could interrupt, Elijah spoke again, his voice steady and calm. "I know you don't like me but let me help you up. I've been in a worse place, and I wouldn't have made it if there weren't people who picked me up. No shame in needing a hand to get back on your feet."

The Judge's lip went tight, and he narrowed his eyes, still refusing to look at the man beside him. This was not going to end well. She stepped closer, intending to send Elijah on his way.

But then the hard jaw wobbled and her father's eyes watered. She froze.

One hand rubbed his face. Her father gave Elijah one quick glance before putting the stern judge expression back in place. "I know you have every right to be here." Each word sounded as if it had to climb over gravel to reach the air. "To see your daughter. I might be weak, but I'm keeping an eye on you. I won't let you hurt them again." He winced as he tried to pull himself up.

She turned away, unsure what to do. Judge Daniels had always been the strongest man she knew. Seeing her father like this made her feel lost.

Hand out, Elijah continued. "I know, and I completely understand. I'm the last person you'd ever take advice from, but don't let pride stop you from asking for the help you need. The consequences aren't worth it. When you have time, I would like to speak with you. I owe you an apology, but the debt I owe your daughter is more than I can pay, so I've turned it over to God. Now, are you going to let me help you up, or will we still be on the floor when your wife and granddaughter return?"

Her father lowered his head.

Elijah went on in a low voice. "Asking for help doesn't take anything away from you. A man who loves his family will let them help. They need to help."

Okay, that turned her lump into a boulder. Turning away from them, she cleaned the counter and checked the mini refrigerator for water.

Her father leaned his head back, eyes closed like he hadn't heard a word Elijah had said.

"Judge Daniels, I'm sure with just a little help you can be in the chair by the time they come back. And then I'll leave. That should make your wife happy."

Jazmine could hear the weary smile in Elijah's voice. Holding her breath, she heard the rustling of movement, followed by slow, heavy footsteps. Her father's recliner popped up and the TV came on.

"So, what are we watching?" Elijah asked. His question was followed by a long period of silence.

"The MLF Championship Cup. Major League Fishing. It's the first round," her father replied in a gruff voice.

Elijah gave a good-natured chuckle. "Yes, I'm aware of that. I know a couple of the guys from Texas. We've been working with the league to get a qualifying event here in Port Del Mar."

"We? Are you back on your family's ranch?"

"My partner, Miguel, and I own the Saltwater Cowboys. We charter fishing trips and tours of the Gulf. Now that my uncle is gone, I've been working with the ranch to expand our reach."

Her father studied his former son-in-law for a bit before asking, "What kind of boats do you have?"

Elijah went into details about his boats and the fishing in the area. Then the men fell silent, watching a high action scene on the TV.

Her father had always been obsessed with sport fishing, a passion she and her mother didn't share. It was one of the reasons he loved the beach house. She quietly made her way to the kitchen and met her mother and daughter heading to the living room.

"Mom, he's watching a fishing show with Elijah. Maybe we should just let him be for now."

"Let him be? The doctor said he needed to rest. How can watching TV with—" she glanced down at Rosemarie "—with your exhusband be good for him?"

"They're talking boats and watching some deep-water fishing show. He's relaxed. Give him room. If you go in all bossy, you'll only upset him."

Her mother lifted her chin and scoffed. "Please forgive me for wanting him to live."

"Mother."

"I'm going to the office to plan our meals for the week. I found a new list with a better variety of approved foods for heart patients. Rosemarie, would you take this fresh tea to your grandfather?"

"Come on, sweetheart." Jazmine put her hand on her daughter's shoulder. "Let's take your papa his tea."

"I don't think he likes tea." The little girl frowned.

"It'll be fine. He loves you, and we'll drink tea all together."

"What about Daddy? Will he want some tea? I can give him GiGi's cup." She glanced over her shoulder. "I don't think GiGi likes him."

"GiGi is very protective of you. She just wants to make sure you're not hurt."

"She thinks he's going to hurt me?"

Ugh. She was making this worse. "No. With Papa being sick, she's just on edge. It'll be okay."

Rosemarie gave a solemn nod.

"It's going to be okay, sweetheart." Together they entered the man cave.

She paused in the doorway. Her father was laying back in his recliner.

"Daddy, Mom went to organize menus."

Her father grumbled something she couldn't make out.

Jazmine decided to ignore him and placed the tea set on the small table between the chairs. Rosie stood next to him.

Elijah stood. "Time for me to go."

"No. You can stay and have tea with us. Please. I have a cup for you too."

His tall frame relaxed back into the large chair, but his nervous gaze locked with hers. "I'm not sure."

She nodded. "Rosemarie helped make the tea. You should try it."

He nodded.

"I want coffee," her father protested.

Rosemarie took a cup from Jazmine and hesitated. Elijah leaned forward and took the cup from her. "Thank you." The smile he gave Rosemarie just about melted her. He took a sip. "Judge Daniels, this is really good."

"Papa, do you want a cup? GiGi says it's good for your heart."

He smiled at his granddaughter. "Then I should drink every drop, right?"

She smiled. "Yes!"

Her father's hand reached out for the cup she held. "Thank you, sweetheart. Oh, look at that big boy." With his good arm, he pulled Rosemarie up into his chair, and she laid her head on his shoulder.

"That's a big fish. What kind is it?" she asked.

Over the last week, she seemed to have acquired her grandfather's love of fishing. Jazmine glanced at Elijah. She'd forgotten how obsessed he had been with the sport. Maybe her daughter had gotten that gene from both.

The three kept their eyes focused on the screen as her father explained everything to her daughter. Jazmine started stripping his sheets and cleaning the area, hoping they would keep him distracted and calm.

Who would have thought that having her

ex-husband in the house would have this side benefit? Gathering the sheets to wash and the dirty dishes, she glanced over at the three sitting in front of the big-screen TV.

Her father chuckled at something and Rosemarie giggled. It was the first time she had heard her father laugh in the last three weeks. "Hey, guys." All three pairs of eyes turned to her. "I'm going to take this up and get clean sheets. Do you need anything from the kitchen?"

"Coffee." Her father was quick to reply.

It was best to just ignore the request so she left the room. In the upstairs office, her mother was tapping away on her laptop. She turned away from Jazmine and wiped her face.

Setting everything down, Jazmine went to her mother and wrapped her arms around her. Azalea had always been a tower of strength. Always in control, never showing any weakness.

Her strong mother crying terrified Jazmine more than anything else since she'd returned home. "Mom? How did the doctor appointment go? Was there bad news?"

"No. No, everything's fine." She slipped out of Jazmine's arms. "Well, the doctor made the mistake of telling him his recovery was going amazingly well."

"Mom, that's great."

"Your father took it as to mean he can do whatever he wants. He is so stubborn. It's like he won't acknowledge he is human and could die. This is the worst time for your ex to worm his way back into our lives."

"Mother, it was time. And you should see them right now. All three are watching some fishing show. Daddy was smiling. He didn't look upset at all."

"Oh. So, you're saying I'm the one who's bad for his heart?"

She sighed. "No. That's not what I'm saying at all, and you know it. You love Daddy and you're worried about him. I am too, but hovering and being overprotective isn't going to help."

She slipped her arms back around her mother. "I love you both so much. Let me help."

Patting Jazmine's hand, Azalea nodded. "I know, sweetheart. If I could, I'd wrap my family in a warm blanket of love and keep the world out. I just want you all to be happy and safe." She twisted and kissed Jazmine's arm. "Will you be okay if I go to the store?"

"Yes! Go. Maybe get your nails done. I'm here so you don't have to do it alone. I know you like being in charge, but you have to take care of yourself if you're going to take care of Daddy."

A few more words and Jazmine left. She gathered up the soiled sheets and went to the laundry room at the end of the hall.

As she went back to the kitchen with the clean sheets, a slight snoring floated from the front room. Jazmine paused at the door. From this angle, she saw Rosemarie hanging on the arm of Elijah's chair. He was leaning in. Their heads were close. She always thought her daughter looked like her other than her eye color, but profile to profile, her resemblance to Elijah startled her.

Jazmine's father was fully reclined and sound asleep.

"Is his heart going to stop working? GiGi said if he didn't listen to her, he was going to drop dead."

Jazmine covered her mouth. Rosemarie had heard her mother's rants.

"I think your GiGi gets mad when people don't do what she says," Elijah replied.

Her daughter nodded.

"It's scary when people we love get sick. Do you know anyone who broke a bone, like an arm or leg?"

"My friend Clare's sister broke her leg on her skateboard."

"She had to wear a cast, right?"

Rosemarie agreed.

"While it was healing, she had to protect it. Then when she got the cast off, she had to rebuild muscles. It took time. That's what your grandfather needs. His heart needs a little rest, a little exercise and a little time. My guess is you might be the best medicine for him."

"But GiGi told me to stay away and not bother him." She frowned and glanced over at her grandfather.

"When he's sleeping let him sleep, but I would say that sitting quietly with him is better than any medicine. Do you do puzzles?"

"I'm good at puzzles. I'm almost six, but I can do some of the grown-up puzzles."

"I remember your grandfather liking puzzles. He likes solving problems and keeping his brain busy. When I see you tomorrow, I'll bring some puzzles that you can give him, and y'all can work on them together."

Jazmine closed her eyes. She and her mother had been so worried about her father's heart that they hadn't thought about him being bored. Rosemarie leaned over the chair arm and whispered something. Elijah brought his head low. He smiled, and Jazmine's heart melted.

She shook her head and went into the room. Going straight to the bed, she popped the new sheet over the mattress. "Sweetheart, it's time for your nap." She kept her voice low so as not to wake her father. Her baby was outgrowing naps, out growing too many things.

"But Momma, Daddy is visiting."

Elijah stood, then knelt in front of Rosemarie. "I have to get back to work. But this has been a great afternoon. Thank you for everything."

Rosemarie glanced at her mother, then lowered her eyes and faced her father again. "Thank you for the doll. I love her. Can I go see your horses? Momma said I couldn't have one, but I could visit them, couldn't I?"

"Rosemarie!" she warned through gritted teeth.

He chuckled. "Of course." He raised his eyes to Jazmine and kept his voice low. "I'll talk to your mom about a time." He nodded and stood. "Okay. Well, this has been a great afternoon. I'll see you soon."

He looked as if he wanted to hug her but shifted uncomfortably. "I'll call later to set up a time."

Moving to stand behind her daughter, Jazmine took her small hands. "If you're willing to wait just a little bit, I'll tuck Rosemarie in with a few books and meet you on the porch."

A moment away from him before they talked

about the next visit was what she needed. Rosemarie's interacting with Elijah was pulling at her heart in ways she hadn't expected. He couldn't hurt her more than he already had, but what if she had to watch their daughter go through the same agony?

She rubbed her head, attempting to ease the throbbing pain.

Chapter Seven

One foot on his front bumper, Elijah flipped his keys through his fingers. He tried to relax against his truck as he waited for Jazmine, but it wasn't happening.

He couldn't tell if the day had gone well or not. His sister's girls were chatterboxes who bounced everywhere they went. Rosemarie seemed far too serious for a five-year-old. He couldn't read her. Other than the moment he offered her a horse.

Then she had called him Daddy. He blew out a gust of air. He had thought his brain was going to implode, or maybe it was his heart. Pushing his hair back, he took a deep breath and tried to stop his shaking hands.

It had been so long since he'd dealt with these kinds of emotions. He snorted and looked upward. A few clouds dotted the light blue sky.

Who was he kidding? He had never dealt with anything like this.

That beautiful little girl with the huge eyes and the serious look was his daughter. He shouldn't be a stranger to her.

The door opened, and Elijah shot his gaze to Jazmine.

She stopped in front of him, a frown on her face. Had he done something else wrong? He swallowed. Fear prevented him from asking.

She crossed her arms over her chest, looking everywhere but at him.

"Jazmine." He bent his head, trying to make eye contact.

She sighed. Meeting him eye to eye, she pinched her lips. "Elijah, I'm sorry."

Sorry. His stomach sank. "Why?" He hated the feeling of not being in control. He'd just met his daughter, but she could be taken away at any time and he had no say in the matter.

"I don't think you coming here is going to work."

His throat locked up. "I...did Rosemarie say anything? Did I do something wrong? I'm sorry about the horse. I can tell her—"

"No. That's not it." A car went by and honked. She gave them a tight smile and a small wave.

The town was already flooded with rumors

that Jazmine was back with his unexpected daughter. The gossips were divided on who was to blame for this scandal. He hated that they were talking about Jazz and Rosemarie.

"Let's go to the back." Without waiting for him, she went around the corner of the house. At the edge of the back deck, she leaned on the railing and looked out to the Gulf. The breeze blew her hair back. A few seagulls flew low and called out, waiting to see if they were going to throw out any crumbs.

"I'm sorry about my mother. I had asked her to stay away until after lunch, but it seems I can't trust her to give us space."

"I could have told you that. For the last six years, they've been fiercely protective of you." He gritted his teeth, not adding that they also kept him from his daughter. Bitterness and defensiveness wouldn't help.

She rolled her bottom lip between her teeth. The moisture in her eyes took the edge off his anger. She was trying to fix this, and it had been his weakness that set it all in motion.

The desire to stroke her cheek was overwhelming. "We'll just have to work around her. She's never going to trust me." He braced his hand on the custom deer guard and leaned back. "What about you?"

Her forehead wrinkled. "Me? I'm doing my

best. I'm just stressed right now. Seeing Daddy so weak has turned my world upside down. But we're not talking about me. I came out here to talk about tomorrow. I also promised Rosie that I'd talk to you about the horse." She cut a hard glare his way. "You realize she will be obsessed until she sees one."

"She can do more than see one. I'm not the broke kid you married. I was serious about getting her one. But it's up to you." He shrugged, hoping to look casual. "We have about twenty on the ranch. More if you count the ones Damian has rescued. There are about twelve we use for the beach rides. All of those mounts are super calm and trustworthy."

Rolling his shoulders, he focused on relaxing and letting the tension move out. "I can set up a ride. We can go out on the ranch or ride along the beach. Your mom can come along." He grinned. "She seems to think I'm going to kidnap Rosemarie. You tell me where and when, and I'll have the horses there." He needed to stop talking.

After a few seconds of silence, she nodded. "We could meet up with you and go riding. For now, we need make it clear she is not getting a horse." Lowering her chin, she glared at him with her best librarian look. "She is not getting a horse."

"What about a dog?" He hesitated to say anything, but he didn't want to be outmaneuvered by her mother. The woman had hated him for too many years to give up now.

She made a noise somewhere between a chuckle and a groan. "You and my mother are going to push my sanity right over the edge. Please don't turn this into a competition between y'all. I can't take any more right now."

Tears welled in her eyes. She opened her mouth but closed it again. Blinking, she turned to the beach and pulled her shoulders forward.

Her pain tore at him. Not touching her was no longer an option. Standing next to her, he wrapped his arms around her and pulled her close.

At first, she tensed, but then she relaxed and leaned into him. The years slipped away, and she fit next to him as if she was his missing piece.

But he had driven her away; there was no going back. He set his chin on the top of her head and watched the waves. Laughter from kids playing somewhere down the beach mingled with the water hitting the sand.

He felt wetness through his shirt. His arms tightened, and he held her closer as she fell apart. She was crying. When she had been his, he would have done anything to stop her tears.

Well, not the one thing that mattered the most. There had been too many nights when she had cried, asking him to stop drinking. That had made him mad. In those days he denied he had a problem.

"It's okay," he whispered. He wanted to tell her he would protect her, but he'd lost that right. He bit back the promises he wanted to make, promises she would see as hollow. Just like the first time he gave them to her.

Closing his eyes, he gently stroked her familiar curls. He prayed for wisdom and strength. "It's going to be okay." Weak, but they were the only safe words he could say. "Your father's strong. He's going to be fine." He brushed his lips against the corner of her temple.

She pulled back, wiping her eyes. A weak smile on her face, she looked up at him. Her dark eyes were bright. He leaned forward. He didn't try to resist her pull.

His gaze stayed deep in hers. Her soft breath mingled with his. The fierce beat of his heart roared in his ears, louder than the crash of the ocean. The world disappeared. The years of destruction vanished. They were young, innocent and in love.

Before he let fear control him instead of faith.

He lowered his head.

Her hand came up and she stepped back, breaking their contact before their lips touched. He let her go.

The sound of the car in the driveway reached him, and Elijah's heart sank. Azalea was back.

Idiot. Where was a concrete wall when he needed to smash his head? He wanted her to trust him, and he did this? He'd never had a strong sense of survival.

Jazmine had moved to the far end of the deck. Her look of horror was a punch to his gut.

Her expression reminded him that it was not his survival at stake. Right now, everything went back to having a relationship with his daughter.

It had to. He wasn't going to be his father; he wasn't going to abandon his family. He would break the family tradition of fathers abandoning their families.

His cousins had made a pact it would stop with them. Xavier was dead, and Damian was so wounded he didn't go to town or make any contact with other people. That left him to break the cycle, and he'd do it no matter what it took. With God as his strength, he could do this.

Being a lousy father was one of many family traditions stopping with him.

His daughter deserved better.

The car engine shut off, and the car door opened and closed. Time was running out.

"Jazmine, I'm sorry. That won't happen again. I'm just here for Rosemarie, I promise. Can I come by for lunch again tomorrow?"

She shook her head. "Why don't we go to the pier? It's public, so my mom won't have any excuses."

"I can make arrangements for us to eat on the upper level. It's for private events. Tell me what she likes for lunch, and I'll have it there."

She blinked a couple of times like she didn't believe him. "Okay. Anything with broccoli and strawberries. They're her favorites. She loves mac and cheese, too. Does the Painted Dolphin still make that?"

He laughed. "Our mac and cheese is the best on the coast. You brainwashed her on broccoli, didn't you?"

She grinned, looking more relaxed. "It never worked with you."

"I've been known to load up on a side of the green stuff every now and then."

"Really? I tried hard enough. I think I experimented with hundreds of recipes, so you would eat healthier." She crossed her arms and looked down. "Elijah, thank you for answering Rosemarie's questions. I had no clue she was worried."

"Sometimes kids don't want to upset the adults they love, so they don't ask. Since she doesn't have to worry about my feelings, I'm safe."

"Thank you for handling it the way you did. It's so hard finding the balance between truth and protecting."

He nodded. Unfortunately, he was one of those ugly truths in his daughter's life. For now, he would focus on what he could control. "So, about the horse. I'd like to tell her our plans tomorrow. Will I be able to take her riding?" He wanted to do something that made his girl smile at him.

The back door opened, and Azalea Daniels stepped onto the deck. "I'm surprised you're still here."

He made sure to smile. He would not let her rile him.

"Mother." There was a warning in her voice.

Great. He grimaced. He loved that Jazmine stood up for him, but he also didn't want to cause friction between mother and daughter.

"We made plans for tomorrow, and we were talking about the best time to go riding at the ranch." She looked back at him. "We just got into town, and she's never been around horses. Let me look at the calendar."

The keys flipped around his finger. "Just tell me when. I have to get back to work. I'll see you tomorrow at eleven."

She nodded.

He tilted his head to her mother. "Thank you for allowing me to visit. I appreciate it."

With another flip of his keys, he turned and got out of there as fast as he could. It hadn't been perfect, but it was a start, and he wasn't going to overstay his welcome.

Jazmine watched him walk away. He had twirled that key ring around the fingers of his left hand. That had always been a sign that he was agitated. Whatever was bothering him, he hid it well. She used to know everything about him. She rubbed her head.

"Are you okay? Did he do something to hurt you? Did he threaten you?"

"No. He was a perfect gentleman." Well, other than almost kissing her, but that had been as much her fault as his.

She turned on her mother. "You promised to keep your distance for this first meeting. I don't want you confusing Rosemarie or making her feel she has to pick sides. It's not fair to her."

Her mother sighed. "I know. But then I started thinking about the night you came to us. You were scared, bleeding and pregnant. My motherly instincts are not going away just because he says he's sober. His family doesn't have a good record."

"I'm not going to let him hurt Rosemarie."

Her mother laid a hand on her arm. "You're a great mother. I'm so proud of you. But you got really good at hiding his drinking from us. I just don't want to see you fall back into that pattern, baby. It's hard to tell your heart to stop loving someone."

"I don't love him anymore." Why did saying that hurt so much?

She turned away and looked at the endless horizon. She understood why her father wanted to come here to heal. Port Del Mar had always been the one place that felt like home, where she belonged. The beach cottage she'd restored with Elijah would always be in her heart.

"Sweetheart." Her mother stepped closer and tucked a loose strand of hair behind Jazmine's ear. "Are you sure he didn't do anything to upset you?"

"No. He just asked to take Rosemarie out to the ranch. He wants her to meet her cousins and go riding." Was she lying to her mother already?

He had almost kissed her. She had almost let him. Was she covering for him again? She couldn't trust herself to be alone with him.

From now on, someone would be with them or they would text. "I'm good, Mom. I think we're just not used to the idea of sharing Rosemarie."

"I'm not sure you should let him take her to the ranch. His family is out there."

"They also happen to be Rosemarie's family. I think it would be nice for her to meet them." She gave her mother a look that made it clear this was not up for discussion. "You know I always wanted…cousins to play with." She had almost said brothers and sisters, but she had had a brother. Even if she didn't remind her mother, it would always be painful, and she had caused enough pain. "He can give her that."

"Yes, well, I think this might be too much for her. It's moving too fast. Too many changes. It has to be hard for her."

She wrapped her arms around her mother's small frame, noticing that she'd lost weight. That couldn't be good. "Change is hard." She leaned her head to her mother's. "If we're truly honest with ourselves, she's going with the flow. We're the ones with all the hang-ups. We're strong and God is holding us. It's going to be okay." Now if only she could believe it.

Chapter Eight

Belle gripped the dashboard. "Elijah, I think she would be perfectly fine with any of our stable horses. They have the best disposition and can be trusted with any level of rider."

It had been a week since his first meeting with his daughter, and each day he got to know her a little better. At first it had been hard to get her to talk. Now he knew all he had to do was mention horses or fishing and the conversation would take off.

Jazz was still dragging her feet about coming out to the ranch, but he wanted to have everything ready when she said yes.

He hit another rut in the old dirt road, and they bounced to the right. He and Miguel had just finished their business meeting with his sister. She had been buzzing with ideas. They'd sell the full Texas coastal ranch experience.

Renting a cabin on a working ranch, cattle drives, riding on the beach at sunset and deep-sea fishing. A Big Texas Experience.

He still thought selling the land would be for the best, but his sister was being stubborn. A family trait.

Their uncle's laziness combined with that stubbornness had put the ranch in financial trouble, but Belle had worked hard to keep it going. After her girls, it was her whole life. Elijah, on the other hand, could've walked away without a single regret. He had nothing but bad memories.

When she had approached him about the partnership, he had one condition—that he could take a sledgehammer to the shed.

She hadn't asked which shed. She had known.

The old wood shed had turned their childhood into a series of waking nightmares. On the nights his uncle was at his worst, he would put them in the shed. Needless to say, they learned to play in silence and stay out of his sight.

Elijah's daughter would never know that the monsters in fairy tales were real. He glanced at his sister. Back then he hadn't been strong enough to protect her, but things were different now. And he needed to keep his head in the present.

After the meeting, he'd told her about Rosemarie's dream of having a palomino of her own. They didn't have one in their line, but Belle thought Damian might be rehabbing one. Their cousin was the true owner of the ranch since Frank had died, but they had grown up more like siblings. Old Frank had been just as mean to his own kids.

Damian was more like a brother, not that it mattered now. Since returning injured from overseas, he didn't seem to care about anyone or anything other than his wounded horses.

Miguel grumbled from the backseat. "Last time I came out here, your cousin shot at me. This is a bad idea. Are you sure he doesn't have a phone?"

Belle laughed. "If he did, he wouldn't answer it. And he didn't actually shoot at you. He would've hit you if he'd been aiming at you. He never misses."

"Oh, that makes me feel better. I know you want to impress your daughter, but she's five. I think she would love that big gray or that little paint pony."

As they pulled into the dirt road leading to the isolated cabin, a tall figure came out and sat in an old farm chair. Tilting it, Damian balanced it on the back two legs, a rifle casually resting across his knees, his beat-up cowboy hat pulled low over his eyes.

Miguel whistled. "How is it a man missing half an arm and leg looks so threatening? Even without the gun, I wouldn't want to tangle with him."

Elijah sighed. "Yeah, he was always the most like his father, but Afghanistan pushed him over the edge."

"No!" Belle turned on him. "He's nothing like Uncle Frank. Just like the rest of the De La Rosas, he's struggling through shadows. He'll find his way if we give him time and support. Just like you needed."

"Point taken." Cautiously, he opened the door and walked to the front of the truck. Miguel and Belle joined him.

"Hey, Damian. Wanted to talk to you about a horse." Small talk would irritate his cousin.

They all stood in silence. The former soldier didn't move, not even to blink.

Belle stepped closer. "Elijah has a daughter who wants a palomino. He wants to surprise her. The other day you had that beautiful mare out in the pasture. She looked perfect. Her previous owner was a young girl, right?"

Damian gave a short nod, then turned his

gaze to Elijah. "Since when do you have a daughter old enough to ride?"

"I just found out about her. She's almost six."

With a thwack, the chair legs hit the boards of the old porch. "Six? You got another woman pregnant while you were still married to Jazmine?" Anger filled every syllable, and his one hand tightened around his rifle.

"No!" All three responded vehemently. Elijah glanced at his sister and friend. It was nice that they had his back.

"Jazmine is her mother. She left without telling me about our daughter, Rosemarie."

Damian frowned and shook his head. He'd been the first one to congratulate them on their wedding. He left for Afghanistan right after Elijah and Jazmine had married, and by the time he'd gotten back, Elijah had been sober again. He'd missed the ugly years.

"While you were gone, I, um, developed a drinking problem. Jazmine decided it wasn't a safe environment for a baby. That's when she left."

Relaxing and leaning back again, he nodded. "Smart woman." He lifted the brim of his hat and looked straight at Elijah. "You sober now?"

"For five years." Elijah wanted to point out that if his cousin bothered to come out of hiding every now and then, he might know what was going on.

One quick nod was all the response he got before Damian hid his face back in the shadow of his hat. "Why me? Why not one of her horses?" He thrust his scarred chin in Belle's direction.

"My daughter wants a palomino. Belle said you have one. If you've trained her and say she's good with kids, I'll pay top dollar for her. I'm not expecting a freebie."

Before Damian had enlisted, Elijah had counted him as more than a cousin. They'd been friends, brothers. They had formed a tight-knit family to protect each other from Uncle Frank, Damian's father.

Now they were strangers. Damian had made it clear he didn't want to reconnect. Didn't want anything to do with people, period.

Like his sister said, the De La Rosas had issues. Some might even call it a family legacy. And this was the family he had to offer his daughter.

"I'm working really hard here to earn father points." He didn't need to mention he was still working on Jazz, but he would have everything in place when she finally agreed. He just didn't know what else he had to offer his daughter. "Is the horse available and good with kids?"

Damian stood, slipping the sling of his rifle over his shoulder like it was part of his arm. Seeing his cousin without the lower part of his left arm still startled Elijah. And by the way the former solider moved, he would never have known the bottom half of his left leg was gone also.

Without a word, Damian stomped across the yard toward the barn. Elijah shot Belle a questioning look, but she just shrugged and followed.

Miguel began walking in the opposite direction, back to the Ranger. Elijah called out to him, but his friend shook his head. "I'll wait by the car. I don't think your cousin likes having people around. I have emails to check." He waved his phone and turned away.

Elijah caught up with them at the tack room. With a bucket of feed tucked into the crook of his arm, Damian gestured at the end stalls. "Don't go near those guys."

Out in the pasture he rattled the bucket, and three horses trotted over. He talked in a low voice to each one as he gave them their treats, then, putting the bucket down, slipped a halter onto a pretty palomino mare.

"She's a little shy and might not ever be trailer ready. Perfect for light pleasure riding, though."

Elijah gently scanned the mare with the palm of his hand. Several areas of her coat were marked by scars. Her front legs were the worst. "What happened to her?"

Belle shook her head. "She was a top prospect with outstanding bloodlines. Poor thing was in a four-car accident. A large truck T-boned the stock trailer she was in. The other two horses had to be put down on the spot. Williams, the owner, was going to put her down, too, but she's his daughter's horse. The little girl was there. She'd been hurt, too. She made her father promise to take her to the vet. They did surgery, but when they informed him she wouldn't be able to perform or carry a foal he said she was useless. Dr. Ryan called Damian. They had to sedate her for the trip to the ranch."

Worried, Elijah studied the sturdy little mare. She rubbed her head against Damian as he talked to her in a low voice. "Is she stable? I don't think Rosemarie has any experience."

Tossing the lead rope over the fence, Damian shook his head. "She's good. If you don't put her in a trailer, she'll be fine. She likes kids."

"Williams just dumped her?"

Damian's hard nod radiated anger, and he petted the mare's forelock.

"She's perfect, just like the horse my daughter showed me. What's her name?"

"Bueno Bueno Sonadora. They called her Dreamer."

"Just like my boats." He stepped back and took a couple of pictures of her. "Nice. Can we move her to the main barn at the ranch house?"

Damian nodded. "I'll ride her over tomorrow and see how she reacts. You got the proper gear?"

"I'll get it."

He moved her to a stall and headed out to the opposite end of the barn, leaving Elijah and Belle standing alone. "I guess that means he's done with us."

"Yep." She squinted at him. "How are you doing? You seem to be taking fatherhood in stride. You are getting legal papers drawn up, right? You have rights as her father. Rights that were stolen."

He sighed and started moving to the door. "Jazmine and I are working this out between us. She'll be in town for seven more weeks. That will give us time to work something out without upsetting Rosemarie."

His sister snorted. "You can't trust her or her parents. They think they're better than everyone else. Or at least better than us."

"She's stronger than she used to be. I had

lunch with them every day this past week. We're going to the beach tomorrow."

She stopped and looked up at him, then threw her arms around his middle. "I'm so proud of you. You're a good man and will make a great father. I know you're already an awesome uncle. When will I get to meet my niece?"

"We're working—"

"—it out. I know. Brother, you need to get something in writing. She can sue you for back child support."

He really didn't want to talk about this right now. Moving to the truck, he adjusted his hat. "I've already talked to a lawyer about child support. I'm going to support my daughter." It made him angry that Belle would even thing he'd try to wriggle out of his responsibilities. She should know him better than that.

Letting go, she punched him on the shoulder. "Stop being a grumpy grump. I know you're going to do what's right. I'm just so mad they think they can keep her from you and then make you pay."

"No one is making me pay. Jazz has already told me not to buy her any more gifts."

She laughed. "And the first thing you do is get her a horse? This is going to be fun." She sighed as they stopped at the front of the truck. "Why wasn't I smart enough to fall in love with a good guy who wants to be a part of his children's life?"

"Don't go there. You're a great mother." His gaze went to the scar on her face. She hated the guilt he carried for her injury. He hadn't protected her when she needed it. "He doesn't deserve the three greatest females on the planet."

His words didn't budge the deep sadness in her eyes.

"These females want to meet your special little girl. She's part of the tribe now."

He let out a long breath. "Maybe they were better off without me. She had good reason to run. Why burden them with the De La Rosa legacy?"

She took a step closer and placed her hand on his forearm. "Now it's my turn to stop you there. We can change the legacy. It starts with us. My girls aren't going to grow up scared and fighting for survival. All they know is love, ours and God's. You have so much to give your daughter." She cupped his face. "You lost Jazmine. But she's giving you this opportunity to be a father, and you're going to be a great one. Our daughters are blessed."

He nodded, but the heaviness in his gut didn't let up. Could he really out run his uncle's legacy? Was it buried in his DNA along with the alcoholism?

Chapter Nine

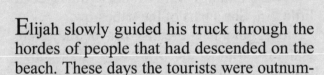

Elijah slowly guided his truck through the hordes of people that had descended on the beach. These days the tourists were outnumbering the locals.

A few of the beachgoers recognized him and waved. This would be the most public place he had taken Rosemarie and Jazmine. All the lunches had been in private areas, out of the way. How could it have been such a short time since his daughter entered his world? It was a world he never expected, but he was anticipating the new adventure.

He tried to imagine if he had been a part of her life from the start. When would he had taken her on her first beach day? She would already know how to boat and sail. Or was she still too young? She certainly could be using the boogie board like a pro. He was by her age.

He had already been riding and deep-water fishing. He didn't really remember learning to do any of that; it had just been part of his life. And it should have been part of his daughter's.

He closed his eyes and ran the morning's verse through his mind. He had to stop thinking about all the "what-ifs" and just enjoy the moment.

All he could do was make this day the best he could. Today Jazmine had agreed to bring Rosemarie to the beach for their lunch meeting, but they were going to meet earlier than normal so they'd have time to play in the sand and water.

A couple of his staffers set up a canopy with chairs, and a cooler full of drinks and food at his favorite spot near the pier.

From the top step leading to the beach, he scanned the area for his ex-wife and daughter. Did Jazmine still wear oversize floppy hats? She had hated the freckles that popped up across her nose whenever she got in the sun. Despite her mahogany skin, any outing would leave her with scattered sun kisses. He had loved them.

She had blamed it on her Irish grandfather.

Her father's parents had always liked him. They'd been the only ones in the family who had welcomed him with open arms.

They had to be in their early nineties by now. Were they still in Austin? He hadn't thought about Jazmine losing her grandparents. A lot could happen in six years. He'd lost his uncle.

Not that the man was missed. But he had also lost Xavier.

He closed his eyes and shot up a quick prayer. Thoughts like that could send him into a bad mental place.

He headed down the steps to the board-walk over the dunes, looking up and down the beach.

He glanced at his phone. It was still a few minutes early. They might not be here yet. He needed to relax.

But then he saw a huge hat with a yellow lemon print scarf fluttering in the wind. They stood at the bottom of the steps, holding hands.

He relaxed. They were here.

Calling to get their attention, he waved as he made his way through the sand. Rosemarie twisted around and waved back.

She stepped closer to her mother and gave him a tentative smile. He had to remind himself that he was still a stranger to her. He couldn't expect her to feel a sudden father-daughter bond just because he did.

It shocked him how much he craved something that he'd never even thought about.

"Hey." He went down to one knee, so they were eye to eye.

"Hello." It was a bashful greeting, but he took the smile as a good sign. It was the same shy smile Jazmine had given him when they first met.

It might be corny, but both females had taken his heart the minute his gaze had fallen on them. There was no getting it back, ever.

Even if Jazz didn't want it.

The love he had for his ex-wife was powerful, but it was nothing compared to the swelling of his heart as he looked into the eyes of their daughter.

This had to be made right. Clearing his throat, he stood and gestured toward the shelter he had his employees set up. "We have everything for a great day on the beach. Shade." He pointed to the oversize bright orange canopy, complete with back drape. "Drinks, food." He gestured to the two coolers. "Sunblock and other essentials. And…" He looked at the large mesh bag. "I wonder what that is?"

"Elijah?" Jazmine gave him a warning look. He could hear the no-more-gifts lecture already starting. But he had five years to make up for.

"What? There are no gifts here. Just essential beach day stuff. Plus, I just arrived, and it was already here. Whose name is that?"

"That's my name!"

He made an act of examining the tag. "Yep. It says property of Rosemarie."

"Elijah?" Jazz didn't sound happy.

He glanced at her. She had her hands on her hips, one brow up and her chin down. Oh man, that glare. It shouldn't make him smile. Smiling was not appropriate. He turned to his daughter, so Jazz's view was blocked.

"It's mine?"

A lightness he couldn't explain came from his core. "Looks like it. Maybe your grandparents sent it."

"Elijah. My parents didn't send it." She looked down at her daughter and tucked a strand of loose hair back in the clip. "Your father is messing with us. He had all this set up for you."

"Really? For me? Can I look inside?"

With excitement bubbling off her, she glanced between Jazmine and Elijah. It was as if she wasn't sure who could grant permission. He wasn't sure either, so he looked at Jazz. She nodded.

He rubbed his hands together. "Okay. Dig in and let's see what kind of activities we get to do today."

With a low shriek, she fell to her knees in front of the bag. Elijah noted with amusement that it was slightly bigger than she was. A gasp of joy erupted as she started pulling out shovels, buckets and molds to build castles. With an exclamation, she held each item up. "Look at this. Oh, look at this one."

Next came a set of horses and little figures, ranging from princesses and pirates to cowboys, all ready to live in the sandcastles. "Wow. There's more." She kept pulling out beach paraphernalia: Frisbees, water goggles and snorkels. "Thank you so much."

Jazz looked at him with one brow raised. He knew it was too much, but Jazz had to understand growing up he hadn't had money to buy even the cheapest plastic shovel.

He held her gaze. "I have so much to make up for. Not just the five years, but everything I never got to give you." He lowered his voice. "I hated not having money to buy you nice gifts. For never being able to get my sister the things other kids took for granted. I don't know what else to give her."

Her eyes softened. "You're enough. I never missed those gifts."

Rosemarie gasped, and they both turned to her at once. "Surfboards?" The toys were spread out around her, and her eyes went big.

He went to his knees in the sand next to her. "They're boogie boards. When you're ready, I'll show you how to use one. We can use them right here on the beach. We don't have to paddle out, so I thought your mom would be happier about that."

She nodded. "Yeah, Momma likes me to stay close." Her head swiveled as she looked at her loot.

"So where do you want to start? Eat first, then play, or play, then eat? We can build castles or play in the water. It's your day, so you tell me where you want to start."

Her eyes were huge. She stared at all the stuff he'd had delivered and looked frozen.

Jazmine went to Rosemarie and sat down beside her. "Sweetheart, I know it's a bit much and it's hard to know where to start, so why don't we eat a little lunch and make sure we drink plenty of water before we start playing in the sun. I think you should start with your dad showing you how to build a sandcastle."

Pulling Rosemarie into her lap, giving her a sandwich then applied sunscreen. "When we were younger, he built some of the biggest I ever saw. Once he made a giant mermaid riding a seahorse for me. When you get hot, he can take you to play in the waves and show you how to use the board."

She nodded. "Okay. Look, Momma, there are three boards. There's one for you, too." She tilted her head up to Jazmine and gave her an unreserved full-on smile.

Elijah caught his breath as a yearning settled deep within him. It hurt. How did he become part of the mother and daughter family?

He didn't have a clue how a real family behaved. He'd never been a part of one. As close as he was to his sister and cousins, they never had a normal experience. Damian had always hated people in general, even before he'd enlisted. He'd never even had a girlfriend. Belle's husband had left before their second child had been born, and Xavier had started off strong, just like Jazmine and him, but never got a chance to finish.

They were a mess. Maybe the Judge and his wife were right, and Rosemarie would be better off without him. Right now, he was an outsider without a clue how to join the circle. Nothing new there.

"Thank you, Daddy." Rosemarie's gentle voice pulled him out of his spiral of negativity.

She smiled at him. It wasn't as big or open as the one she'd shared with her mother, but it was a smile.

He hadn't thought it possible to fall love even deeper. The time was going too fast. How would she remember him after they went back home so soon? In a short time, she had managed to change his life in ways he could have never predicted. She changed him.

"It's like an early birthday." Picking up a horse and shovel, she looked ready to attack the sand.

Turbulence rocked the pit in his stomach. He didn't know the day she was born. Where had he been while…he closed his eyes. "When's your birthday?"

"August seventeen."

He stopped breathing. Three weeks after his. They would be gone by then?

Stay in the present.

"This is not a birthday gift." He flashed a worried glance at Jazmine. "It's not even a gift. Just some stuff everyone needs on the beach. Let's say it's for all of us. So what do you want to do first? Your mom can rest here in the shade if she's too tired to play."

Crossing her arms, Jazmine rolled her eyes. She had always done that, right from the first day he'd met her.

Grabbing a cold bottle of water out of the cooler, he tossed it to her, then handed one to Rosemarie. "The sun is high today, so make sure to drink plenty of water." He jutted his chin toward one of the chairs. "Sit, relax, enjoy the view. We're going to build a giant castle for your royal highness." He winked at her.

Rosemarie ditched the horse and grabbed a bucket. "I want to build a castle in the sand. Will you help me?"

"That's why I'm here. That looks like a good spot to build. What do you think?"

With a nod, she ran to the area and dropped to her knees. He turned to Jazmine. "Are you going to join us?"

She shook her head. "I'll guard the mother ship. You have fun with her."

He looked at Rosemarie already digging and making a pile, then back at Jazz. "Has she said anything about me?"

"Go build the sandcastle. You're good at being a big kid. I'm giving you this time to spend with her. Do what you do best. Go play."

He glanced at his daughter, then back to his ex-wife. "Why don't you come play with us? You look like you could do with a little fun." Judging by the look on her face, that was the wrong thing to say. *Smooth move, De La Rosa.*

She shifted in her chair and glanced at their daughter. "Being responsible for another human being is serious business, Elijah. Spend time with her. Talk to her. Listen to her. I'm going to read, but we will be leaving in two hours. Use your time wisely. Get to know your daughter."

"You were always too serious."

"And you always needed to grow up."

He bowed in defeat. He headed out into the sun, then stopped and turned back. "I've made arrangements for us to go horseback riding on the ranch. There's a horse that's perfect for her. Would Friday work for you?"

"Elijah, I'm not sure she's ready to go horseback riding."

He snorted. "She's a De La Rosa. She was born ready to ride a horse."

"We're here on the beach to spend time with you. Right here, right now. We'll talk about future plans later."

"I don't want to break any promises to her. Please don't make me a liar."

"You told her about getting a horse before talking to me." The wind snapped her hat back. As she went to grab it, her paperback fell off her lap.

He stooped to pick up the book. She reached for it at the same time. Instead of grabbing her book from the sand, he held her arm and looked up at her, then back at the scar running from her palm to the underside of her wrist.

His brow furrowed. That hadn't been there the last time he saw her. A knot squeezed his gut. His thumb softly traced the jagged line. It had been cut with something uneven. "How did you get this?" His brain screamed at him to not ask. He didn't want to know. After a long stretch of silence, he forced his chin up and held her gaze. "Jazmine?"

Pulling her bottom lip in between her teeth, she broke eye contact with him.

Sand clogged his throat. "Jazz?"

She glanced at him, then swung her eyes to Rosemarie. "What do you remember from the night I left?"

He had to fight the urge to go out and get lost in the waves. Facing his past actions, his mistakes, was never easy.

No matter how much the denial screamed in his skull, he had to hold steady and listen. He took a deep breath. "Not much. When I woke up, I was on the sofa. My laptop was in the yard. The front window was broken. Chairs were turned over and…"

That was the worst day of his life. Waking up to the mess he knew he had made but couldn't remember how it had all played out. He could only imagine. "The table was turned over, dishes broken on the floor. The big mirror you loved was shattered into a million pieces. There was blood, but I had a few cuts and bruises, so I thought it was mine." He tightened his fist and looked down, recalling the bloody cuts across his knuckles.

Please, tell me it was mine. He sat back on his heels and ran his fingers through his hair. "It wasn't mine, was it?"

She shook her head, a sad smile on her face like she was apologizing. "I had made a special dinner to give you the news about…" A tear slipped down her cheek.

He didn't want to hear this. "That night. You knew you were pregnant?"

Head down, she gave him a quick nod. "Yeah. I had called you to make sure you were coming home. You said you'd be home in less than an hour. I waited. A storm blew in, and I was so afraid you'd stopped off at the Watering Hole. I knew if I could just get you home, the baby would give you a reason to stop drinking.

"A few hours went by and you hadn't shown. The storm got worse. I was worried about you being out. I called several times, but it went straight to voice mail. I didn't bother to leave a message. I fell asleep on the sofa."

"Oh, baby. I'm so sorry." He wanted to cry for the pain he had caused, the joy he had destroyed. All the time he had lost.

The worst part? He didn't even know what had been so important that night that he hadn't gone home to her. There were a few bars he had visited. The people were faceless, nameless. He'd given himself to them instead of to the woman he had promised to love and cherish. The mother of his daughter. His gut hit a new low.

"About two you stumbled in, mad about something. I couldn't understand what you were saying. I was upset because this had become your normal. I told you to leave. That if you wanted to spend your nights with Will and Tristan, you could spend your days with them, too."

He wanted to touch her. To give her the comfort he hadn't given her that night.

"I told you the drinking had to stop. It was out of control. You were out of control. The anger was so intense. Then you turned your back to me."

She took a deep breath and watched Rosemarie. "I was standing right behind you. Reaching out, I touched your shoulder." She closed her eyes. "That's when you clenched your fist and smashed it into the mirror. On the reflection of my face. I was shocked. I'd never seen you violent. You know my parents never even yelled. I was so scared."

She had only been nineteen, and pregnant. His gaze went to their daughter, blissfully playing in the sand. Because of Jazmine, none of his ugliness had touched their innocent little girl. She was an incredible mother.

"I told you to stop. Instead, you went on a rampage. You hit the wall again. That was your blood on the walls there. You flipped the table, and then you threw your laptop through the front window. You were yelling that my father had ruined your life. I ran to our room and locked the door. You banged on the door, yelling at me to unlock it. I told you to leave. For about thirty minutes—it seemed so much longer—you ranted. Elijah, for the first time ever, I was afraid of you."

He couldn't hold back any longer. He placed his hands on her knees. "Jazz, if there was any way in the world I could go back and change that night—that year—I would in a heartbeat. There is no way I could ever express the..." He lifted his head. "There are no words, nothing I can do to erase that night." He ran his thumb over the bunched scar tissue. "How did this happen?"

She shifted a little away from him and watched Rosemarie play for a while before continuing.

"You finally passed out. After I was sure, I opened the door and crept into the living area. You were face down on the sofa. I think I was in shock. The mirror. A present from my parents. The rage I saw in your eyes right before you smashed my reflection was something I had never seen and didn't ever want to see again."

Tears landed on his skin. He wasn't sure if they were his or hers.

"All I wanted was to put the pieces back together. I went to my knees and tried to gather the broken shards of glass. Somewhere inside I thought if I could fix the mirror I could..." She shook her head. "The tears started falling so fast I couldn't see. You made a noise. I jumped, thinking you had woken up. I cut myself. The blood was all over. I couldn't stop it. I got a towel from the kitchen and went to my parents. I didn't know what to do. Elijah, I had never been afraid of you before, but with your uncle's history..."

Lifting her chin, she looked at Rosemarie. Their daughter was pressing sand into molds.

He nodded. "I get it. After my aunt died, my uncle got worse. We decided to send Gabby away to her mother's sister. She was only eight, but it was the only way we knew to protect her."

"Gabby?"

"Yeah, she's the baby of the family. Xavier and Damian's little sister."

Tears hovered on her bottom lashes. All the

pain in those eyes had been put there by him. "I hated my uncle. I wished I could have sent my sister away. You did what you had to do to protect our daughter."

Now he looked at the tiny little human he had helped create. She stood and danced to the other side of the mountain of sand. A few other children stood close, like they wanted to play but didn't know how to ask.

She caught his gaze and waved at him, her smile open and honest. There were no clouds of pain or hurt in her eyes. He realized at that moment that he had to let go of all the anger he had been holding on to.

He looked back to the mother of his child. "You did what you had to do to protect her. You are an incredible mother. She has no clue how blessed she is to have you. Is there anything I can do to... I don't know? I want to make your life better. I can't do enough to make this up to you and her."

"Elijah, you don't have to work so hard for her to like you." She closed her eyes and leaned her head back on the chair. "Go be with your daughter. I need to be alone right now. We'll talk about the horse later."

He glanced down at the book in his hand before handing it to her. "So, you haven't stopped reading your romance novels. Does that mean you still believe in love?"

"It's fiction." The lack of emotion in her eyes tore at his heart. He was the reason for the emptiness there. She took the book. "It's an escape that my heart needs. My daughter is my focus."

He nodded. "I want her to be my focus, too. Please let me put Friday in the books. Belle can have everything ready at the ranch. There'll be a horse for each of you."

"Your persistence must be why you've been so successful at your business."

"Sorry. I just need to do something, and she wants a horse ride." He wanted to tell her that the business didn't mean anything to him; it had just given him something to do. He had been so lost without her, but it wasn't fair to her to lay his pain and guilt at her feet. "I want her to meet her aunt and cousins. They want to meet her."

With a heavy sigh, she glanced over at their daughter. "Be at the house, Friday at 5:30. A short ride. Maybe just around the barn. She's never been on a horse before. So small steps. Okay?"

"Okay," he quickly agreed. "After we ride, we can make ice cream with peaches at the ranch house." He smiled, remembering all the nights he had made her ice cream with fresh peaches. She had joked that the treat was the reason she had fallen in love with him. He'd given her too many reasons to fall out of love. Pushing out a hard breath, he looked at the sky and cleared his thoughts.

"I'd like her to see the family place."

An unladylike snort escaped Jazmine. "You hated your family's ranch."

"It's better with my uncle gone. There's not much to give her when it comes to my family history, but it's a part of her history, too."

She glanced at her phone. "You're wasting time talking with me when you should be talking to your daughter. Go build a castle. Friday we'll go riding with you."

"Daddy! Come help me."

He needed to stay focused on his daughter. The days were flying by in a rush. The limited time had to be used wisely, to make a permanent bond with his daughter, so that when they went back to Denver he'd still be a part of her life.

Jogging over to her, he went to his knees.

"Daddy."

"Get ready to make the biggest castle ever." Picking up a shovel, he pushed it deep into the sand. His heart absorbed the sound of her joy, and he thanked God for the gift he had been given. He needed to enjoy the moment and not think about the things he couldn't change.

Jazmine had done what she had needed to do, but now she was back, and he was sober.

God had given him a second chance. He might not deserve it, but he wasn't going to waste it.

He invited the kids who had been hovering to join the fun. He knew the parents of one of the boys. The girls giggled in agreement when Rosemarie explained how the cowboy had to be saved by the princess.

He glanced at Jazmine. Her eyes were focused on her book.

She had been his princess, but when she had tried to rescue him, he had pulled her into the riptides instead.

He thanked God that her parents had been there to get her out of his mess. They deserved his respect and appreciation.

Jazmine stared at the pages of her book, but the words just floated. Glancing up at the small group of children that had gathered around Elijah, she saw her shy daughter laughing as she played with children her own age. She looked like she belonged, instead of hanging around the edges watching the fun.

Elijah had done that for her. His charming,

easygoing playfulness came so naturally to him. Early in their relationship she had told him he'd be a great father. Even now, she remembered the look of horror on his face. The thought of having children had terrified him.

Looking back, she had probably added to his stress every time she'd mentioned wanting children.

He'd been so afraid of becoming his father or uncle. But she had assured him that he was so different from them. To her, he had always been a man of honor, one who loved deeply.

She had to take her gaze off the man. Instead, she turned her eyes to the endless horizon. The Elijah she needed to remember was the one who had started drinking.

Not the boy she fell in love with, the one who taught her to embrace life and dive into the water, to jump from the pier and dance with joy. She had lost him to alcohol. The addiction and his family legacy had swallowed him in their undertow.

Watching him with the children, with their daughter, she saw the man she had thought he could be. With the castle high, his little fan club added shells to the turrets and towers. A couple of boys finished the moat and let the water come in with the tide. A cheer erupted from the group, who laughed and clapped as the water rushed in and surrounded the grand castle.

Rosemarie ran to the canopy. "Momma, did you see it? It's the biggest one ever!" She grabbed the bag with the rest of the toys. "We're going to put the other people and horses in it, then Daddy's going to show me how to stand on the board. Are you going to do it, too?" She bounced with excitement as she gathered up all the toys Elijah had bought her.

"No, sweetheart. I'm going to watch from the shade." Jazmine picked up a bottle. "Before you go, let me put more sunblock on you."

"It was nice of Daddy to get us shade, wasn't it?" Rosemarie lifted the curls off the back of her neck, so the lotion could be reapplied.

"Yes, it was very thoughtful of him. Now go play—you only have an hour left before we leave."

"But I don't want to leave. I have new friends."

"No arguments, or we can leave now." She looked over at the other kids. "I'm sure your father knows some of their parents, so we can invite them over."

"Can I invite them to my birthday party?" She sounded like her father.

By then they might be back in Denver. "We'll talk about it later. Go play."

With a heavy sigh, Rosemarie bounded off to her father and new friends.

Jazmine prayed her daughter wouldn't get hurt when it came time to go back to Denver. Would Elijah still be so eager when they were out of sight and the newness had rubbed off?

Elijah ran to the water, waving for the kids to follow. His laughter had all the children running along with him. Her heart seemed ready to jump back in, but she was smarter this time and wouldn't follow.

If he had really found his faith and left the drinking behind, maybe she could stick a toe in to test the waters.

Every child deserved a chance to have a loving father in their life. She closed her eyes. *Please God, protect my baby girl's heart.*

If she was honest, her heart might be at risk, too.

Chapter Ten

Elijah gritted his teeth. Miguel had called from one of their boats out in the Gulf. Ben, one of their best captains, was in trouble. He'd been sober for eighteen months, but now he was drunk at the Watering Hole and was trying to drive himself home.

The owner had called Miguel instead of the cops, and in turn Miguel had called Elijah. He'd done this before.

With a quick glance at his watch, he calculated how much time he had before he was scheduled to pick up Rosemarie and Jazmine. He could get Ben home, then take his daughter out to the ranch for her first ride.

Crossing the threshold to the old dive had his skin crawling over his muscles. The dim lights of the bar hid the grunge and sadness.

The smells turned his stomach. *God, let me get in and out as quickly as possible.*

More than five years had passed since he had been a patron. There was nothing pleasant or temping about his old hangout. This place had distracted him from his real life. The pressure from her family and his uncle had been his focus instead of Jazmine. He had hated the life he thought he was supposed to be living. But the beautiful parts had been lost too, because of fear.

He spotted Ben by the jukebox, arguing with Patrick, the owner. When the short man saw him, relief flooded his face. "Elijah! See, Ben, I told you he would come and get you home. You don't need to drive."

Ben's red-rimmed eyes glared at him. "You said Miguel was…coming." He tried to turn away and fell against the jukebox. "I don't need no help. I can…drive just fine." He stumbled in the other direction.

Patrick shook his head. "He won't give me his keys."

Elijah nodded and put his hand under Ben's arm. "Come on, buddy. Let's get you home. When Miguel gets off the boat, he'll stop by for a visit."

"I can't go home. She won't…" The man started crying. "I promised—" He fell to the side.

"I'll take you to Miguel's place, okay?"

The older man nodded.

At first it went smoothly. Ben followed him to the parking lot. When Elijah opened his passenger-side door, the older man fell apart. Deciding he was being kidnapped, Ben made a run for his car, yelling and screaming.

With a heavy sigh, Elijah went after him.

Arms wide, Ben tried to swing at his rescuer.

"Ben, I'm here to help you."

Another swing.

Elijah managed to duck, then tackled the man against the car. "Give me your keys so we can go home." Not knowing where the man's keys were, he was carefully guiding him toward his Ranger when Ben's fist punched him in the center of his gut.

Being so unsteady on his feet, the older man didn't create much of a threat. Even so, he managed to get another shot in, right on the bridge of Elijah's nose. *Great.*

Miguel and Ben owed him big-time.

A patrol car pulled into the lot, blocking Elijah's vehicle. He sighed. This was just getting better and better.

Officer Sanchez approached them. "Everything all right?"

"Oh, peachy. Just trying to get ol' Ben to Miguel's place safely."

"Sounds like a good plan. Need help?"

Ben finally relaxed and let Elijah take him to the passenger's door again. "Thanks, but I think we got it."

This time he was able to open it as the drunken man leaned his head against the side of the Ranger. He was clearly giving up the fight.

Pulling out his phone, Elijah checked the time. Not too bad. If he could get the older man home, he'd be only a few minutes late. One arm braced against Ben's chest to hold him in place, he scrolled and found Jazmine's number.

A strange noise came from the man next to him. Before he realized what was happening, Ben had leaned into him and lost his last meal.

With a yelp, Elijah leaped back, dropping his phone, but it was too late. His shirt was covered. Bending down to rescue his phone, he gagged. Lying on the filthy pavement, his phone was even in worse shape. The screen was broken.

Officer Sanchez laughed. "No good deed goes unpunished."

"Thanks," Elijah growled. There was a towel in his backseat, but it wasn't much help.

Ben leaned into Elijah. "I'm so sorry," he mumbled.

Sanchez went to his car and returned with a plastic bag and a T-shirt. "Here. Put your phone in here. The shirt might be a bit small for you, but it's clean."

"Thanks." Elijah made a fast job of taking off his once favorite tee and tossed it in the plastic bag with the useless phone. It was history. He'd have to get a new phone in the morning. "Come on, Ben, let's get you home. I have a date with a very special lady."

Sanchez raised an eyebrow. "Really? And you came here to save this old coot?"

"Yeah, he wanted to drive. Not going to let that happen."

As Elijah buckled Ben into his passenger seat, Sanchez clapped him on the shoulder. "I don't care what anyone says, you're a good man, De La Rosa." The officer laughed at his own joke.

Elijah grunted. This was a good reminder of why he was sober. He had a date with his daughter. That lifted his heart.

He waved to Officer Sanchez, then glanced at Ben, now snoring against his window. He'd drop him off, then head over to pick up his family.

Hopefully, he wouldn't be too late.

Thank you, God, for the reminder and the opportunity to be that little girl's father.

Jazmine placed the dry dishes in their proper places and resisted the urge to look at the time again. Elijah had worked too hard for this day to show up late. He owned several businesses now, so maybe something had happened. Bracing her hands on the edge of the granite counter, she dropped her head.

Did she really just start making excuses for him? He had a phone.

"Momma! What time is it? How much longer until he'll be here?" There was the sound of a truck outside. Rosemarie ran to the window and looked out. She turned around with a pout. "Did he say what kind of horse I was going to get to ride?"

"I think he wants to surprise you." She broke and glanced at the clock. Fifteen minutes. Her heart plummeted. He had been early to every appointed time.

No. He said he would be here. She wasn't going to panic. He'd be here. She was just on edge because she was going to have to tell him something that would upset him. "Do you have a change of clothes?"

"Yes." Rosemarie bounced and twirled. "He

said my cousins would be there. I've never had cousins before. Did you know I have five, but three are babies? They're triplets, like twins but there are three of them. Zoe and Claire are twins, but there are only two of them. Three at one time. I've never seen triplets. Have you?"

"Only on TV." There had been a time it was challenging to raise one baby by herself. But triplets? She couldn't even.

Elijah and Xavier had been so close. It had to be difficult to know he wasn't coming back to his children.

"It'll be fun to have cousins." Rosemarie had gone back to her perch on the window seat.

Jazmine went to the window and stood behind her daughter. She had worked so hard to protect her. If he did anything now to prove her mother right, she'd...well, she wasn't sure what she'd do, but he would regret it. No one hurt her baby.

And he was going to have to deal with her and Rosie going back to Denver sooner than expected. It wasn't going to change anything other than the daily lunches. She was doing the right thing taking her daughter back home. Getting back into a routine was good for a young child.

Restless, Rosemarie ran to pick up her horse and pack it in her bag. "Maybe my horse will be a palomino." Zipping up the bag, she skipped around the table, excitement bouncing off every part of her body. "Maybe it'll be black, like Black Beauty."

Tires crunched the crushed gravel in the drive. With a squeal, her daughter ran to the window. "Oh." Her tiny shoulders dropped, right along with the excitement in her voice. "It's just GiGi and Papa."

"How about we pack some snacks and make Papa's tea?"

Rosemarie skipped to the pantry and pulled out her favorite snacks. "Should we get some carrots and apples for the horses?"

"I'm not sure." The door slammed downstairs. She had hoped they'd be gone before her mother and father arrived. She made the tea, trying to keep her heart from pounding with each passing minute.

After a minute her mother's heels hit the stairs, but before she reached the top she hollered up. "Jazmine, come down here. I need to speak with you in private."

She closed her eyes. Dread filled her. After giving Rosemarie a task to keep her busy, Jazmine gave the clock one last glance, then made her way to her mother.

"What's up, Mom?" Her mother's tight face didn't ease her anxiety.

"I saw him. It's not good." Azalea crossed her arms.

From his recliner, her father scowled. "Jumping to conclusions is a waste of time, honey. We should have stopped to see if he needed help."

Eyes rolling high into her brows, Azalea shook her head. "I know what I saw, and you needed to be home to rest." Her gaze bored into Jazmine. "Has he called?"

"No." Jazmine hated the hesitation she heard in her voice. "Did you see him?"

With a nod, Azalea narrowed her eyes. "In the Watering Hole parking lot. He couldn't stand straight. Looked like he was fighting with someone. The police were pulling up as we sat at the red light. It didn't look good."

Her gut twisted. All the old memories of waiting for him swamped her.

Hearing the Ranger outside, they both turned toward the door. Her mother crossed her arms. "Do you want me to tell him to leave?"

"No. I'll talk to him." She had made a promise not to run and hide behind her parents. She met him at the door. His hair was disheveled, and the shirt he wore was too small. It was obviously not his.

"I can't believe you drove here."

Frowning, he looked at his truck, then back

to her. "How else would I get here?" He walked closer to her. "So sorry I'm late. Are y'all ready?"

"Do you really think I'm going to let her go with you like this?"

"What?" His eyes went wide. "Wait. You think I've been drinking?" He stepped closer to her.

She stepped back, repelled. The smell. It was as if they had slipped back in time to all the nights he had showed up late and lied to her. But it was worse. He was lying to their daughter now. He was making their daughter wait.

She forced herself to step out of the house and close the door. "I can't believe you would come here like this. And you drove."

He blinked, a look of confusion on his face. The exact same look he used years ago to pretend he hadn't been drinking. "Jazmine, I haven't had a drink. I had… Well, I went to help a friend. I didn't think it would take this long, but it got complicated. And even if I was drunk, I'd never drive. You know that."

"I don't know anything." She waved her hand. "This situation was so complicated you couldn't call or text?"

He reached out to her, his eyes burning. "Baby. Listen to me, please. I haven't—"

"Don't." She wrapped her arms tight around

her middle. She had been so stupid. "I know that smell all too well. I'm not doing this. I'm not putting my daughter through this."

Biting the inside of her cheek, she willed back the tears. Crying over him was in her past. It wasn't going to happen again.

"Jazz." He looked up to the balcony, then back to her. "I'm not drunk. I know how—"

"Stop. For all I know, you've gotten worse. Maybe you even drove back then. I was so naive I believed anything you told me. I won't go there again."

Taking his cowboy hat in his hand, he slammed it against his leg.

She jumped.

"Right." He dropped his head and pinched the bridge of his nose, then winced.

Was that a bruise?

He took a deep breath and looked back at her. "There was an emergency. I couldn't just ignore it. Yes, I went to a bar. The Watering Hole. I had to go inside. Someone got sick, and I had to borrow this shirt. I didn't go home and change because—"

"Daddy?" They both looked up to the balcony above them. "Can I come down? Are we leaving?"

With a big intake of air, Jazmine forced a

smile. "So sorry, sweetheart. There's been a change of plans."

"Jazz, please don't do this." His voice, low and gravelly, made her want to believe him. Forgive him. "I'm less than thirty minutes late."

"Your dad just dropped by to tell me he doesn't feel well."

"Jazz." He closed his eyes and gritted his teeth for a moment before putting that wide smile on his face. "So sorry, sweetheart. We can't go today."

He was blinking, and his breath was coming in quick pants. "I promised her."

She would not, could not give in to him. "Don't make promises you can't keep." She forced each word from between clenched teeth.

He put his hat back on and ran the back of his hand over his eyes.

His eyes were cold. And, she realized, clear. There weren't glassy or hazy, but stone-cold clear. Without breaking eye contact with her, he spoke loud enough for Rosemarie to hear. "We will be riding on the ranch before the month is up."

Her mother joined Rosemarie on the railing. "I'm so sorry. I thought she was in her room. I'll take her inside." She put a protective arm around the small shoulders. "Goodbye, Elijah."

His eyes went colder. "She saw me at the Watering Hole, didn't she?"

"Don't blame her. She wouldn't have seen you there if you hadn't been there."

"So instead of asking me why, you jumped to conclusions." He took a step back. "I'm not going to argue about this. If you can't listen to me right now, I need to walk away. But I promised Rosemarie a ride, and we are going to make a new time and date."

He turned and walked toward his truck.

Why did she feel like she was in the wrong? He'd been the one to break promises. "You can't just make plans without my approval. Before you do anything, call me."

He paused but didn't turn around. "I've lost your number. Call the Painted Dolphin and leave it with them so I can put in my new phone."

"New? What happened to your phone?"

He opened his door. "I'm sure you wouldn't believe me. I'll have my lawyer contact you. We can set up all future dates through her."

"Are you threatening me?"

"No." There was a deep sadness in his soft voice. He finally turned. "I'm setting boundaries. We both need to come from a place of respect, and if we can't, a mediator might be a good idea." He paused at his opened door.

"I'm leaving now because I'm not going to fight with you. I'm not going to try to make you believe something you don't want to believe. But I want to be very clear about this— I am not walking away from our daughter."

Slipping into the truck, he shut his door and backed out of the drive.

Everything in her told her to run after him and…what? Apologize? She didn't have anything to be sorry for. He had slipped into his old ways, and she wasn't going to be an enabler this time. She had done her own coddling. Without knowing it, she had helped his addiction. She was smarter now, stronger.

But his eyes had been clear, part of her brain insisted. It didn't matter, she argued with herself. Even if he was sober by the time he drove out here, it was obvious where he had been. She couldn't afford to disregard the warning signs and explain away his actions.

She should feel strong, so why did she want to throw up? She glanced at the balcony where her sweet, innocent daughter had been standing. Her fears had come to life. Elijah was so easy to love when he was sober. But what she remembered the most was the waiting.

All alone at their house, waiting late into the night. Waiting for him to reach out to her when she had moved to Denver. All the waiting had hurt her so deeply.

Now her daughter was hurt.

Elijah gripped the wheel. His jaw hurt, and his breathing was short and shallow. Did he really expect her to trust him?

Yes. Without trust, how would they be able to parent Rosemarie together?

He'd jumped through all her hoops. Then the first time he'd been a little late she'd slammed the door in his face. The urge to stand and fight, to yell until she listened to him, was strong.

But he had done the right thing. He slammed the steering wheel. He wanted to show her the phone. Wanted to drag Sanchez up there so he could explain. He wanted her to believe in him. But he couldn't force her.

Even now, he wanted to go back and say more. The words he wanted to scream swirled around his head. He wanted to force her to listen. But force was never the right answer.

She didn't trust him, and he couldn't make her feel something she didn't. His knuckles twisted.

If Miguel hadn't called him to get Ben… *No.* He wouldn't start the blame game. Pulling into the barn area, he rested his head on the steering wheel. *God, how do I fix this?*

His gut hurt.

His sister stood at the barn door and waved with a huge grin. Her girls came out and ran to the truck. They were excited to see Rosemarie. Family was so important to his sister.

But there was no Rosemarie. His eyes burned. No way was he going to cry, but the pain was deeper than any he had felt in a while. He had already missed too much of his daughter's life. There had to be a way to fix this before they left, but if Jazmine wasn't going to have any faith in him, he was fighting a losing battle.

Confusion marred the faces of three of the most important people in his life. They glanced into the truck and then back at him.

"Where's Rosemarie?" his older niece asked.

"Elijah?" his sister asked, her hands resting on his open window. "Where are they?" She frowned. She leaned in and sniffed. "And why do you smell like..." Her nose wrinkled. "Is that cigarette smoke?" Horror flared in her eyes as she stepped back. "Girls, go inside."

Leaning his head back against the headrest, he closed his eyes. *Great.* Not only had he upset Jazmine and disappointed Rosemarie, now he had upset his sister and nieces.

Lord, help me change the things I can, accept the things I can't and give me the wisdom to know the difference.

"Elijah, what happened? Tell me, please, because right now I'm scared to death."

Opening his eyes, he studied the face of his beautiful sister. Together they had been through so much. Life had taught them early on that the people you love had the greatest power to hurt you. And yet here she was, still willing to love him.

He looked into her eyes as the story spilled out, swallowing his raw emotions. Here was the one person in his life who would believe him and be there without question, the way family should.

All he wanted to do was love his daughter the way his sister loved him. Loved her girls. Now all Rosemarie knew was that he had broken a promise.

Had he been an idiot to think Jazmine might ever trust him again? She had once, and he had crushed her.

Chapter Eleven

Jazmine caressed her daughter's hair as they watched a movie with her parents. She shoved down her desire to go to her room to cry for Rosemarie's sake.

A pounding on the door jerked all their attention from the TV. Moving Rosemarie to the side, Jazmine rose and went downstairs to answer it.

Outside stood Elijah's sister, Belle. Her eyes were red. Fear spiked Jazmine's stomach. Stepping out of the house, she carefully closed the door behind her.

"Is Elijah all right?" What if something had happened after he left? Maybe she had read him wrong and he hadn't been in any condition to drive. She should have called someone to pick him up.

"No. He's not all right."

Jazmine gasped. Her hand flew to her mouth. All the blood dropped to her knees.

"You made him break a promise to his daughter. You kept her from him for her whole life. And now you...you take away a day that he's been planning with so much detail. He's been working so hard to make sure everything was perfect for her."

Relief flooded her body. "He wasn't in a car wreck?"

"No! But you might as well have run over him."

Pressing her palm to her forehead, Jazmine closed her eyes. She wasn't in the mood for this. "Belle, this is between Elijah and me. I'm not—"

"Stop. He told me not to get involved, but after everything he's gone through, everything he's fought through, I'm not going to let you hurt him where it matters the most. I'm going to tell you that he's a great uncle, and he'll be the best father ever. You don't have the right to take that from him."

Belle jabbed her finger in the air. "He was keeping a drunk off the road. He might not be used to fatherhood, but people in this town count on him."

"What?"

"He has become a depend—"

"No, no. What was he doing tonight? How can he be keeping a drunk off the road if he's the—"

Belle threw her head back and grimaced at the sky. When she brought her chin down, a fire was burning in her gray eyes, so much like Elijah's. "You punished him for doing the right thing. He hasn't touched a drop of that stuff in over five years." With a sound of disgust, she turned away and looked at her phone.

The door opened. Jazmine jerked around, afraid of seeing her daughter. Instead, her mother stood there. She wasn't sure if that was any better. "Mom, please go back inside."

Her mother's face made granite look soft. "No. His family doesn't have the right to harass you."

Belle turned back, her chest expanding as she stepped closer, her finger pointed. "You don't have the right to keep his daughter from him." Her eyes grew moist. "She has a whole family that wants to know her and love her."

Azalea sniffed. "A family that can't be trusted."

Elijah's sister stood taller. "He is not our uncle." Her chin lifted. "You don't know my daughters or…you don't know us."

"Mother, stop. Insults are not going to help. Belle, I'm sorry."

Jazmine turned to her mother. "She was saying that Elijah was at the bar to stop someone from driving drunk."

Belle nodded. "His phone was ruined in the shuffle. I can tell you that he's never late, and he hasn't had a drink in years."

"Mom, you said you saw him fighting with someone and the police were there?"

Taking a deep breath, her mother closed her eyes and lowered her head. "The police were pulling up. I assumed." She raised her head and looked at her daughter. Her skin had lost some of its color. "I... He was struggling with an older man I didn't recognize." She pressed the back of her fist to the bottom of her chin, her eyes darting as if she was looking for something. "Your father warned me about jumping to conclusions. If he was stopping someone from driving drunk, why didn't he say that?"

Jazmine groaned. "I didn't let him, and what he did say I refused to believe. I didn't want to..."

Azalea crossed her arms. "I just don't want to see my daughter hurt again. And Rosemarie is so innocent. As a mother, you should understand that."

Belle's stance softened. "I do. But I've seen Elijah work so hard to overcome our family's past. He knows how personal it is to your family. He'd never allow anyone to get on the road if they've had anything to drink. He never has, even at his worst."

Azalea glanced at Jazmine.

She nodded in agreement. "It's true, Mother. He'd walk home on the nights he…" The memory clogged her throat. She swallowed. "I'd go get his car in the morning while he slept it off. He never drove."

Belle reached out, the fire gone. "Your first instinct is to protect your baby. But you don't have to protect her from Elijah." She smiled. "I might have also gone a little mama bear protecting him. He asked me to stay out of it, but I told him I had to run to the store."

Azalea stepped closer and put her arm around Jazmine. A girl was never too old for her mother's hug. "Is it too late for Jazmine and Rosemarie to go for that ride?"

"Elijah is at the barn with my girls."

"I'll call him." Jazmine's heart picked up as she reached for her phone.

"You can't. His phone was ruined. Believe me, it's a complete goner." Reaching into her back pocket, Belle pulled out her cell. "My oldest has a phone. We can call her." She dialed, and they heard the ringing through the speaker.

"Hey, Mom. What's up?"

"Tell Tío Eli that I ran into Jazmine and she wants to speak with him."

They heard a gasp. "Are they coming?" Excitement colored each word.

"Hand the phone to your uncle."

"Izabella, I told you to stay out of this." Elijah's voice had no give in it.

"Do you want to take your daughter for a ride today?" She looked at Jazmine with a tight smile. "Talk to her and don't be *terco*."

"I'm not being stubborn." His sigh was heavy. "Is she there now?"

"I'm here. I'm sorry about earlier. I should have at least given you a chance to explain." She was proud of herself for keeping her voice calm and steady.

"Oh, hi. Sorry. I thought I was still speaking to Belle." Unease lined his voice.

She couldn't help but chuckle. "Yeah. She handed you to me. So, she explained the situation to us. I'm sorry we jumped to conclusions. I should have known you wouldn't have driven to the house if…well, you know." Fire ants attacked her stomach. "Would it be okay if we followed Belle out?"

"We're at the barn, and if you get here in the next twenty, we should have enough daylight."

"Good. We're on our way." Her throat was dry. "Elijah—"

"You need to head out now if we're going to get to ride. We'll talk later."

"Okay. We'll talk later. See you in a bit."

She handed to the phone back to Belle. "Looks like we're going riding."

Her mother nodded. "Let me get Rosemarie. I know she did a good job of hiding her disappointment, but this will make her very happy."

Belle moved to her Jeep. "As soon as y'all are ready, we can head out."

Jazmine nodded. She wasn't sure she was ever going to be ready to have Elijah back in her life. Her emotions were too unpredictable.

He had taken a shower in the tack room. His skin scrubbed clean, Elijah smiled at Lucy and was about to answer one of her many questions when Belle's old Jeep came into view. It was followed by a small, shiny SUV. He hadn't allowed himself to believe they were actually coming.

After the showdown in front of her house, he'd thought it was over. That he would have to fight with a team of lawyers to see his daughter again.

But she was here. Somehow his sister had made this happen. His throat tightened. After all the years of him being a walking mess, she had fought for him. Even at his lowest, she had been there ready to kick him out of his wallowing self-pity. She had been an unabashed example of tough love.

Now she was bringing his daughter to the ranch. She was his role model for parenting, not the man who raised them.

Her girls clapped. "Rosemarie is here!"

He grinned. "Where should we take her? To the pasture or the beach?"

They both jumped up. "The beach. The beach."

His sister stopped the Jeep right next to him. She hopped out of her vehicle and grinned at him like she'd brought in the winning catch.

He leaned close to her ear. "I told you to stay out of it."

Not a hint of guilt or apology touched her face. "And if I'd stayed out of it? Your daughter wouldn't be on the ranch. You've worked hard to get your life right. They can't treat you like dirt. Not as long as I'm around."

"Not only do I not have credit with Jazmine, I'm digging myself out of emotional bankruptcy. I owe her. She has every right to do whatever she thinks is necessary to protect her daughter."

She reached up and tugged at his ear. "Your daughter. How long are you going to punish yourself?"

He started to reply but shut his mouth. She

wouldn't accept his answer. The sweetest sound saved him from having to think up another response.

"Daddy!" Rosemarie yelled, as she plowed into him. "We made it! Are you better?"

"Yes, and I'm so glad this worked out. Are you ready to meet my new horse I just bought?"

"She's yours? Yes!" She screamed and clapped. "What's her name?"

"Bueno Bueno Sonadora."

She made a face. "Good Good something? That's a strange name."

He laughed. "Sonadora means dreamer. You know Spanish." That surprised him.

"I'm learning at school. Why does she have two goods in her name?"

"Bueno is very important in the quarter horse bloodlines and she has it on top and bottom, so they put it in twice. That's the name on her official papers. I'm thinking of giving her a new name. What do you think? The little girl who had her before called her Dreamer."

Her little nose wrinkled. "Top and bottom?"

Laughing, he lifted his hand above her head. "The father's side of the family is listed on top." Then he tickled her at her waist. "Her mother's family is listed on the bottom of her papers."

She flung her arms around him again, erasing all the unpleasantness of the past few hours. He forced himself to stay in the moment. No worries about the future or guilt about the past.

Jazmine joined them.

Rosemarie turned to her mother and clapped. "Momma, did you hear? Daddy has a new horse. Where is she?" She was bouncing with barely controlled energy.

Cassie and Lucy each grabbed one of her hands. "She's in the barn." The girls took off running.

"Slow down," all three adults yelled at the same time. Belle rushed ahead to take the girls into the stables.

Picking up the pace, Elijah followed, but a warm touch on his arm stopped him. He looked down at the stern face of his ex-wife and gave her his best smile. "I've got the horse covered. It's been a long time since I've had my own horse. She's going to stay on the ranch, and I'll share her with Rosie. Please, Jazz, let me do this." His gaze sought out his daughter. "The only good moments growing up were with the horses." He came back to Jazmine's eyes. "It's the only thing I have to offer."

Her fingertips brushed his chin. "Not true. And that's not the point. You said you were going to find a horse she could ride, not buy a new one. Why do I have a feeling you will never ride this horse that you didn't buy for your daughter?" She sighed.

He took her hand and walked to the barn doors. Her hand fit into his so naturally. "Let me tell you her story. Her owners wanted to put her down, but Damian saved her." He gave her all the details. "She's a sweet horse, a bit shy, but with a great deal of love to give. She just needs the right little girl. They're a perfect match."

Stopping, she pulled him around. "Elijah, how am I supposed to say no to that?"

On impulse, he kissed her forehead. "You're not." *What was he doing?* Taking a quick step back, he released her hand, then turned to follow the girls.

The three cousins were standing at the far end of the breezeway. His heart paused. They were here as a family. He stood behind them, his hands on the tiny shoulders of his daughter.

Belle led the mare out of her stall and Rosemarie went still. She seemed to stop breathing and a strange sound came from her. Had he done something wrong?

He bent down and pulled her against him so that her back was pressed against his chest. "What's wrong, baby?"

She shook her head. "She's beautiful. Just like in my dreams." Twisting, she looked up at him. Wet with tears, the gray eyes looked violet. "Is she really ours?" The small voice was filled with awe.

"What are you going to call her?"

"Dreamer."

"That's perfect because she knows it already."

She sank further into his chest. "What if she doesn't like me?"

He couldn't imagine anyone not loving his girl. "You belong to her now. She needed a little girl just like you. She was in a bad accident and has scars, but she's all better. I bet she's nervous about meeting you."

"Think so?"

"I was the first time I met you. Remember?"

And today he'd almost lost her. One mistake and he would lose everything again, but this time there was more at stake. It wasn't about him, or even Jazmine.

He glanced up and made eye contact with Jazz. He had to be strong and make the decisions that were best for his daughter. And Jazz. No matter how much he loved them, he had to put that aside and do what was best for them.

Chapter Twelve

Jazmine hung back. This was the kind of moment a little girl would remember for the rest of her life, and Elijah was making it happen. He had always been that way. Zeroing in on a person's dream and making it feel like it could come true.

Belle stopped in front of them and smiled. "Dreamer, this is Rosemarie." The pretty mare lowered her head, and the little girl gently touched the soft muzzle. The horse made a rumbling noise in her throat. Rosemarie giggled.

"Ready to saddle up? Girls, get your helmets." Belle was all business.

Out back, several other horses were already saddled and waiting. Elijah went step-by-step, showing Rosemarie how to saddle a horse and take care of it. Lifting her into the saddle, he explained each action before leading her to a large round pen. Belle and her girls followed on their horses.

"Your Tía Belle is an excellent horse trainer and riding instructor. One of the best in the state. She's going to help you before we hit the beach. I'll take your mom to get her horse. You okay?"

She nodded, a huge grin on her face. She leaned forward on her mare and hugged her neck.

As they started through the doors from the barn to the arena, they saw Damian standing at the other end.

"Wow. I wasn't expecting to see him," Elijah said. "Hey, Damian. What brings you out?"

He tipped his hat. "Wanted to make sure the transition went well for Dreamer and Rosie."

Smiling, Elijah turned to Jazz. "The only person better with horses than Belle is Damian."

"Hey!" His sister's voice carried across the arena. "I heard that." Belle sidestepped her horse to open the gate and lead Dreamer into the arena. "I mean, it might be true, but you don't have to say it in front of me and my girls."

"It's okay, Momma." Lucy urged her mare into the arena. "We already know Tío Damian is the best with horses, but you're better with people."

Elijah laughed. "Out of the mouths of babes."

Belle shook her head. "Whatever. Go get yours and Jazmine's horses. I've got this covered."

"Yes, ma'am." He patted Rosemarie's thigh. "Relax. Have fun and listen to your *tía* and *tío*. Your mom and I will be right back with our horses, and then we'll all head to the beach."

He turned to Jazmine. "You want to stay here with her? I'll go get our horses."

"No. I'll go with you."

"Are you sure? I know you don't like Rosemarie out of your sight."

She snorted. "First, I'm within shouting distance. Second, your sister is raising two girls on her own, and they seem well-adjusted and happy." She winked. "Remember who taught me how to ride? She was one of the best back then, too."

"True." His sister had the trophies and ribbons to prove her skills.

"Anyway, I need to talk to you."

He paused as he slipped the halter off the buckskin's ears. "Talk about what?"

She took a deep breath. The comforting smell of hay and salt air soothed her. "Daddy is being an overachiever, as usual. The doctors said his recovery is ahead of schedule."

"That's great news, right?"

"Yes. Absolutely. But I think that means it's time for Rosemarie and me to go home."

He leaned on the saddle he'd just cinched and looked at her, his eyes wide. "What? I thought we had more time?"

"I want to get her home and back into a routine before school starts." That sounded weak even to her own ears. Was she just running again?

Without a word, he picked up the other saddle and placed it on a bay's back. His muscles bunched and moved across his shoulders. "Is this because of the bar incident? I thought we were good."

"No. I was going to tell you today." She waited for him to say something.

He wasn't responding. Of all the scenarios in her head, his silence was not one of them.

"I'm missing work. I don't want her to lose connections with her friends. Elijah? What are you thinking?" Did she really want to know? She put a hand over her stomach, trying to calm it down.

He had his back to her. hands were braced on the saddle. "We're supposed to have more time together."

"You knew we would be going back."

He shook his head. "At the end of summer. She's just getting comfortable around me. You're worried about her forgetting her friends in Denver. What if she forgets me?"

"She's not going—"

"I'll move to Denver. I'll get a condo."

"Elijah, you can't just leave here. Your dreams have always been tied to this place, and now look at you. Those dreams have become reality. You've worked so hard. This place is in your DNA, just like the color of your eyes. It's a part of you."

He finally turned. "She's a part of me I didn't even know was missing. Building up the business has kept me focused on something other than everything I lost. She's bigger than all of those put together and there is so much to make up for. I don't have to be here every day to run the business."

Her stomach twisted. She hadn't thought of him moving to Denver. He'd be part of their daily lives. He walked the horse over to her and handed her the reins. His hand brushed hers and she wished the moment could last.

Standing in front of her, he studied her face. There were so many unidentified emotions pinging through her head.

"You don't trust me. I got the message loud

and clear today." He turned from her and, in one quick motion, mounted his gelding. "Or is it that you don't want to share her? You've had her to yourself for almost six years. Are you running again? I understand why you don't trust me, I get it. But how much of you leaving is to keep control of my relationship with Rosemarie?"

"What happened earlier today was not fair to you. You have been nothing but trustworthy." To the point that she was having a hard time remembering why she needed to stay away from him. Maybe she was running. It would be too easy to give her heart to him again, but could she trust him? Could she trust herself?

Stepping into the stirrup, she swung her leg over her horse's back and settled into the saddle. The bay shifted under her.

The truth? She had left her heart with him, and her parents knew it. That was the reason they had worked so hard to keep her away from him.

But if all the changes she had seen in his life were true, there was no reason to run from him again. He was right. She had run last time, and she was about to run again.

Offshore, thunder rolled. The sunny day disappeared fast as storm clouds were propelled in from the Gulf. They had made it only a mile before the weather changed on them. Announcing they needed to head back, Elijah was met with a chorus of groans.

After rubbing down and stalling the horses, they ran for the screened porch that covered the back of the ranch house. They almost made it before the heavens opened.

Belle pulled out towels for everyone as lightning flashed across the sky. The girls laughed and recapped their ride, not realizing how dangerous the weather had become.

Elijah jumped as he felt a heavy hand on his shoulder. Turning, he found his sister. Belle's brows were pulled tight.

"Everyone's fine and we made it safely to the porch." Taking his hand, she squeezed it between both of hers. "I know the storms bring back the worst memories, but he's gone. He can't hurt us anymore. Don't give him the power." She pointed her chin toward the girls, now sitting with Jazmine. "Relax and have fun."

They would never know the fear of being locked outside during a storm or sleeping in the mud as rain poured into the shed they were locked inside. Their childhood would be filled with joy, love and adventures. Storms wouldn't bring the monsters out of the shadows, because they wouldn't have monsters there to begin with.

"Knock, knock!" His cousin's widow, Selena, opened the screen door from the kitchen. "Room for a few more?" She carried one little boy on her hip, his straight dark hair falling over his gray eyes. Two more with identical wild curls toddled out ahead of her as she guided them like a mother with three arms. The two on the ground squealed when they saw Cassie and Lucy.

"We heard a rumor that I have a new niece, and the boys wanted to meet her." She tried to set the one she held on the floor, but he clung to her and buried his face in her hair.

Selena hugged Jazmine with her free arm and introduced her sons. Elijah went into the house and helped Belle gather the ingredients to make ice cream. Cassie and Lucy showed Rosemarie how to add each item to the ice cream maker. Female voices and children's laughter filled the porch as the rain hit the metal roof.

Selena cut a bowl full of fresh peaches.

Elijah sat back. The women in his family were so strong. He was the weak link. Ben was an ugly but true reminder of who he was at his core. He had failed. When Jazmine and Belle had needed him, he had been drunk.

He was one drink away from being that guy again. He wasn't two separate people, the good guy versus the jerk. They both lived in him.

Rosemarie ran to him with two ice creams in hand. "Did you see? We made real ice cream. Here's yours." She took a bite of hers, and her eyes rolled back in bliss. "This is so good, Daddy. Momma said this is why she fell in love with you."

Jazz bumped him until he scooted over. Sitting next to him, she nodded. "How can a girl say no to a man with homemade peach ice cream and a barn full of horses?"

Rosemarie giggled, then ran off to join her cousins.

They sat next to each other as they watched the kids play on the porch. Two of the triplets kept trying to run out into the storm. The other was forever hiding his shoes under something. Selena finally gave up on covering his feet, but she refused to let the children out. They turned their attention to the litter of half-grown pups in a playpen. The girls took the pups out and total complete joyous chaos ensued.

"Jazmine."

Her large eyes turned to him as she took another bite of her ice cream.

"Thank you for making sure Rosemarie..."

He didn't know how to put what was in his heart into words she would understand.

"Elijah?" She lowered the ice cream cone as she looked directly at him. "What is it?"

"You've given Rosemarie a childhood and home that is full of love. You made sure she was safe. Thank you."

"It's what any mother would do."

"No, it's not. I didn't even know what a home was until you made one for us. I'd never belonged anywhere. My mother didn't stay around to make sure we were okay."

He'd had a tough childhood, but… "I knew your mother left you, but you had a home. You had your sister and cousins. Despite your uncle, y'all seemed so close."

"We were. We needed each other to survive." Another roll of thunder vibrated the house as lightning flashed.

She held his hand. The warmth anchored him. The kids laughed and crawled into the daybed with the puppies.

He couldn't look at her. "I never wanted you to see me as less because of the way I grew up. I didn't have a bedroom. Most nights I wasn't allowed to stay inside the house."

She gasped. "You never said anything about being forced to sleep outside. That's child abuse. Why didn't anyone intervene for y'all? Where did you sleep?"

He shrugged and kept his voice low. "We were De La Rosas. We were written off as damaged goods." His jaw hard, he looked down, then tilted his head back and scrutinized the ceiling as if it held the answers. "On a good night we slept here on the porch or in the barn. Sometimes he wouldn't let us stay there, either. Storms made him worse. We made sure to stay out of sight during storms."

All the moisture left her mouth as she sat next to him, perched on the edge of the bench they shared. His worst nights had been during storms.

"When we disobeyed orders, he had a toolshed he'd lock us in for periods of time." He turned to face her. "I'm not telling you to make you feel sorry for me. I just want to be honest about everything. Part of the reason I drank was the shame..."

Instinct made her tuck his arm against her and pull him close so there was no space between them. The need to comfort him drowned out all other worries. Her fingers wrapped around his. "But that's your uncle's shame. Not yours."

A rough grunt was followed by a lopsided

grin. "At the very least it was embarrassing. You came from such a perfect family."

"Elijah, no family is perfect. A child is not responsible for the actions of the adults in his life." Running her hand up his arm, she squeezed. "There was no way you had done anything to deserve that treatment."

"In my head I know that. But here—" he tapped his chest "—is another story. That's part of what I had to learn. I'm dealing with it."

"You hated your uncle, so why did you stay in Port Del Mar? You had to fight my parents and him to build a life here."

Rolling his shoulders back, he shifted away from her. "I've always liked a challenge." His sarcasm wasn't missed.

"Some might call it stubbornness." She let her dry tone match his but followed it with a wink.

"Yeah. That's a trait the De La Rosa family had in abundance."

"Hello, have you met my mother? Poor Rosemarie didn't have a chance. There were times I wasn't sure if we'd survive the terrible twos, and then she hit the threes." Both of their gazes went to their daughter. "Man, those made the twos look easy. She was awesome at saying no, but if anyone dared say no to her, she could bring the roof down with her fits."

He frowned. "She was difficult? She's so sweet and shy." His expression had relaxed. Rosemarie was letting a puppy lick her nose as she giggled.

"Will you tell me more about her as a baby and toddler?"

Jazmine smiled. "She's my favorite topic. Around new people and places she is very shy, but once she's comfortable, watch out." She told him of the period when Rosemarie refused to wear clothes. Then about the battle of eating anything other than chicken nuggets. Her obsessions with horses and purple. He asked questions and laughed at the more outrageous stories.

The smile on his face was warm and relaxed. "Okay. So, she's sweet, shy, smart and stubborn. All the best *s* words. I wish I could have been there."

"You're here now, and you'll be there for her in the years to come."

Years? The thought of a forever promise terrified him. Another spiderweb of electricity flashed through the clouds as thunder rolled over the land. The girls jumped and screamed, then fell into bouts of laughter.

While they were on the beach, the storm had come in unexpectedly. What if he hadn't gotten them back to the house in time today?

Damian might have the right idea. His family was safer with him watching from the perimeter.

If he made a mistake or a misstep, the collateral damage would be too high. Should he even get a house in Denver? Jazmine's instincts had been spot-on the first time, so why was he trying to stop her from running now?

Chapter Thirteen

Jazmine took a deep breath as she let the quiet of her car soothe her. Ten minutes ago, she had pulled up to the beachside cottage she and Elijah had bought just months after they had married.

With Jazmine and Rosemarie leaving for Denver soon, Elijah had wanted to make dinner for them tonight in the home they had built together.

The home they built together. The words had bumped around in her head since he said them. They had made promises to each other, and the only thing that stopped them had been his drinking, which he acknowledged and turned over to God. So, what was stopping her now?

For over twenty-four hours, she'd rehashed the same dialogue with herself. Her heart pounded as she sat in the car looking up at the warm lights shining out. This was where their love had grown and died. The best and the worst had all happened here.

Since she'd been back, God had shown her the best could still be theirs if they both trusted Him. Now she was about to change their course again, if Elijah agreed.

To her surprise, her father supported her. Her mother hadn't said anything one way or the other but had agreed to keep Rosemarie tonight so that she could talk to Elijah about their future.

She'd even bought a new sundress in his favorite color.

Her barely there sandals hit the first step, and she looked down. The wooden deck and all the old loose boards were gone, replaced with all-weather decking. There hadn't been enough money for upgrades back in the day.

The seaside cottage sat high on the exposed pilings. It was smaller than her parents' beach house, but the first time she saw it from the beach she dreamed of making it her home. Before they were married, she had told Elijah it should be theirs.

She had fallen in love with the wraparound deck. The turquoise blue she had picked out looked fresh. It was a bit of a shock to see he had repainted the deck the same color. The corners of her mouth went up, easing some of her dread.

It had taken her a while to convince Elijah that the color was perfect. It still looked good on their little beachfront house. The white trim had recently been redone, too.

Her knees shook so hard she had to slow her pace. When her parents said the house had been sold in the divorce, she had cried. It made the end of their marriage more real than anything else.

The outside looked the same, but the inside had to have been changed. Had other women picked out furniture or rearranged her dream home? She stopped.

This had been a mistake. If other women had been in her home, she'd be sick. Maybe she should meet him somewhere else.

It had been six years since she had left him, but she had never really thought about Elijah moving on without her, never thought of him building a new life inside the shell of their old one. It should have been expected, though. He was young, good-looking and now a success-ful business owner.

Laying her hand on her heart, she tried to calm its rapid beating.

This was their house, where their family be-longed.

The idea of restoring their relationship had

been planted in her brain that day on the ranch. Or maybe it was in her heart. Her heart had gotten her in trouble before. But her head also told her they could have the future he'd promised her over seven years ago.

Standing on the deck wasn't going to get anything done. Closing her eyes, she cleared her head. *God, I'm turning this over to You. I know through You all things are possible, and if he has put You first, then we can do this. We need You to guide us through these choppy waters.*

She stood and smoothed out the nonexistent wrinkles in her soft pink summer dress, then adjusted the starfish necklace.

The windows glowed with warm light. Her heart slammed against her chest. This time, they could get it right.

Raising her fist, she paused. Her bracelets slid down her wrist. On the anniversary of their first date, he had given her a bracelet made of natural stones. He had promised to give her one each year.

She smiled at the pretty pieces of jewelry. Six were missing. But those six years might be the most important to their future. They had needed that time to grow up and find the strength to trust in God.

Before her knuckles hit the textured glass.

Elijah opened the door and stepped back, a huge smile on his face and a dish towel in his hand. "Sorry, I didn't hear a knock. Have you been here long? Come in." He looked behind her. Frowning, he stepped onto the deck and looked around. "Where's Rosie?"

"I left her with my parents."

He closed the door, confusion on his face. "But I thought we were having dinner together. Is something wrong?"

She played with the bracelets on her arm. "No. I just wanted to talk with you alone. Talk about our future."

"Our future? With Rosemarie? I don't understand." He rubbed his palm against his worn jeans. A look of deep fear burned in his eyes. "Have your parents—"

"No. No. It's nothing like that. I think this is good news. I hope it's good news." Now she wasn't so sure of herself. This had seemed so much easier in her head. Needing to center herself, she scanned the living area that used to be her home. The fear of seeing changes had made her avoid really looking around.

What she found startled her. "It looks the same."

It was a large open room that flowed into the white kitchen. An island anchored the space between the rooms. The four stools she had found at an estate sale were still there, waiting for the family she had always imagined.

The cream sectional was new, but the same style. The pillows had been replaced, too. But they were still the fun, tropical colors and patterns she had y spent hours selecting.

She turned slowly, taking in every detail. "You haven't changed anything."

As she took in their old living space, her hand went to her heart. There had been a few new additions that brought tears to her eyes.

Photos of Rosemarie were framed and placed around the living room. The drawing their daughter had made for him after their horse ride hung in the dining room.

Even the lopsided ceramic cup that she had made at Sunday school was on the island holding scissors and measuring spoons. Seeing her daughter's work in the home she had decorated so many years ago tightened her heart and twisted it into a lump of emotion.

Moving to the island, he draped the town over the edge of the sink and kept a wary gaze on her. "I loved everything you did here. Growing up, well, you know. For the first time, I had somewhere I belonged." He looked at her. "A place that was made for me."

Until he had told her the horrible events of

his childhood, she hadn't really understood his need for a home.

"For you and our children." Sitting on the stool across from him, she reached over and took his hand. "Is this why you stayed here instead of leaving? You could have started over somewhere new." Like she had done. Instead, he had stayed and fought for the dreams they had shared. Now she knew without a doubt she was ready to fight alongside him.

He stood, walking to the sink. "I couldn't leave. Too many people needed me. Belle's husband left her. Then we lost Xavier. Selena discovered she was pregnant with triplets." One hip pressed against the edge of the counter, he turned to the window, as if studying something out in the darkness only he could see. His shoulders tensed as though the weight of the world was getting too heavy.

"They needed me. Honestly, I had thoughts about leaving." His gaze sought her. "There was a part of me that was hanging on to the idea that you might come back. I had to let that go. There were times I thought I'd be better off selling and starting over."

His chest expanded as he inhaled deeply. "The absolute truth? When we first started dating, I didn't think I deserved you. I thought that once we were married I could relax. You'd be mine, right?"

She slipped onto the stool and nodded.

"But even then I was afraid you would realize I wasn't worth the hassle. Fear drove me to hide in the alcohol. Your parents wanted me to be more. They made that clear when they got me the job in the law office. I hated every minute of it. But I couldn't tell you."

"I never expected—"

"I know. I'm not blaming you or them. It's just what was in my head at the time. You needed someone better than me. I tried and, as we know, it didn't work out so well."

Both of her hands went to her mouth. "Elijah."

With a sigh, he crossed the kitchen, out of her reach. "I fought to keep the house because of you." He ran his hand over the butcher-block countertop. "The house was a reminder that you saw something in me you could love, even if it was for a short time. I lost control of my life, and I lost you because I was living in fear and hiding—or trying to hide." Bracing his hands on the edge, he lifted his head and studied her for a minute.

His half-cocked grin melted her heart.

"Reclaiming my life was not easy. During the darkest days of my battle, the house became a touchstone. When my uncle's voice got too strong, our home reminded me that, through God, I was worthy of love."

There was no stopping her tears as his honest emotions tore at her. Needing to gather herself, Jazmine turned away from him to do something, anything, to get control of her heart and brain. Heading to a cabinet by the front door, she paused. The world shifted under her feet.

She couldn't be seeing what was there, propped against the wall, tucked safely between the two tall cabinets. The mirror.

Fingers outstretched, she touched the hand-carved frame. Lightly stained wood surrounded the six-foot mirror. It was warm under her touch. Her parents had commissioned the custom mirror as a wedding gift.

She looked up and met Elijah's steady gaze. Silently, he had crossed the room. Now he stood right behind her, just like that night. Instead of being lost in a haze of alcohol and rage, she found concern and doubt clouding his beautiful face.

"How?" The word came out as a strangled whisper. "You destroyed it that night." Breaking eye contact with him, her attention went straight to the front window he had broken during his fit. There had been a fierce storm that night. She focused on him again. "It was shattered."

His throat worked for a second. "Yeah, I wanted to fix the original, but…" He shook his head. "I took it back to Omar, and he did the best he could. It needed new glass."

Caressing the smooth wood, she allowed her thoughts to travel back to their wedding day. The joy, the endless promise of a future full of love. Then she noticed the new inscription. Jazmine dropped to her knees to trace the letters. "Psalm 40:3. What verse is that?"

Elijah lowered to his haunches, next to her. "'And he hath put a new song in my mouth, even praise unto our God.' I had to learn a new song. That's why I put it here, by the door, so I see it every time I leave."

Silence fell between them. He reached over her shoulder to touch the frame next to her fingers. The warmth of his skin was so familiar, even after six years. His scent surrounded her.

One slight move and she could bury herself in his arms. With a tilt of her chin, she looked up at him. His lips were so close. His gaze lowered to her mouth. All breathing stopped as her heart pounded hard.

The back of his knuckles gently caressed her cheek. Tears. He was wiping off tears.

His fingers moved up into the curls of her hair, and the years between them slipped away.

The warmth of his hand rested on the back of her neck as he pressed his lips to the small area between her ear and jaw. He knew all her sensitive spots. He knew her. He brushed her hair from her shoulder and trailed soft, gentle kisses to her chin.

Finally, he reached her mouth. She leaned in and, for an instant, their lips touched. Her hand went to his arm to balance herself and pull him closer.

Instead, cool air hit her. He was gone.

Opening her eyes, she found him standing a few steps back.

"Elijah?" She waited for an explanation. Something. Anything.

Heavy wrinkles marred his brow. "I'm sorry, Jazz. That can't happen. I promised myself I wasn't going to do anything to complicate our relationship. Once something is broken, there's no getting it back. Rosemarie is the most important person in this scenario, not our old feelings."

"What if they're new and stronger?"

A pained expression crossed his face. With a hand in his hair, his arm rested on the top of his head. One pivot and all she had was his back.

"Elijah?"

He groaned. "Feelings are not my strong point."

"But that doesn't mean you should ignore them."

"Parenting is the only thing between us from here on out." The timer went off, and she was ignored as he set the roasted chicken on a cooling rack. In silence, he pulled a couple of plates down and fixed them. Sliding a plate in front of her, he sat on a bar stool one space over. He stabbed a piece of broccoli. "So, you came here without Rosemarie, but you claim I have nothing to worry about." He stared into the night, chewing with too much energy. "Just so you know, I kind of worry all the time now."

So many emotions were whirling around her heart and head she couldn't sort them out. He had built a new life without her. Just like she had in Denver.

The only reason he had let her in now was because of their daughter. The daughter she had kept from him. Was that too big for him to really forgive?

What if she had gotten this all wrong and he didn't want her, just Rosie?

Chapter Fourteen

Blinking her eyes, she cleared her thoughts and focused on what he was saying.

He adjusted his napkin. "God had to start from the ground up with me. There isn't a day that's easy."

The jellyfish were back in her stomach. She pushed the chicken around. That night six years ago was so clear in her head, but how had the following days played out for him?

She had been in survival mode, allowing her parents to take care of her and all the decisions. She had focused on her baby, on creating a new life for them in another state. At nineteen she had still been a child playing house.

Letting her parents remove any means of contacting Elijah had eased the stress and uncertainty that surrounded her decisions about him. They knew his voice alone would soften her. What if she had been strong enough to reach out to him a month or two later?

He grinned. "What are you thinking?"

"How did you... I mean when did..." She took a deep breath. "The next morning? What happened after you woke, when you found me gone?"

He stood up, his gaze focused on the wood floors.

"Do you remember?" She slid onto the stool closer to him, but he shook his head and moved farther away.

Dinner forgotten, he went to the sofa and sat, his arms resting on his thighs, his head down. "I remember every detail."

His head came up and his gaze crisscrossed the room, as if he were replaying the morning in his head. "At first I rushed through the rooms. The times before, no matter how late I came in or what I did, you were still here. I was terrified. No matter how hard I concentrated, I couldn't remember anything after leaving the bar.

"I panicked until I noticed all your things were still here. Your hair stuff and makeup littered the bathroom. I thought maybe you'd gone to get more coffee. Or you went to get my car. You did that a lot, too."

His gaze stilled on her. "I took it for granted

you were just cleaning up my mess again. I was so self-centered."

He closed his eyes and leaned his head back on the sofa.

A long moment of silence let the images of that night sink into her thoughts. "All I did before I left was cover the window. The rain was coming in hard and pooling on the floor. I didn't want our new floors to be ruined."

His attention stayed on the white beams above them. "It looked as if you'd be right back. So, I thought I'd help." He grunted. "The great Elijah started sweeping up all the scattered debris and broken glass. Could I have been more of a clueless idiot?"

She bit her lip, holding back a snort. "I might have thought the same thing a few times."

He nodded and gave her a half-hearted smile. "I assumed you just needed cooling-off time. After an hour or so—" he gave a hard, self-deprecating laugh "—I tried calling, but you didn't answer. Then I called your parents. At first they didn't answer, either." He searched her eyes for a heartbeat. "Did you ever get my messages?"

"No. I gave my phone to Mom and told her not to let me answer. Monday, they gave me a new phone and number."

Moving across the room, she sat on the wicker

chair next to him, she reached over and took his hand. "I'm s—"

Brows knitted, he frowned at her. "Don't say you're sorry. I'm the one who put you in a place where you were forced to do that."

Leaning forward, she lightly squeezed his fingers. His free hand started tracing the old scar at her wrist. Instinct told her to pull away, but she held still.

"Your mom finally answered and made it clear I shouldn't call again. You weren't my business anymore. I was sick to my stomach thinking of how I had treated you. I understood that you needed time away from me."

He stood, breaking their contact. Behind the sofa he began rearranging the colored glass bottles on the smooth driftwood shelf. "I put everything back in order and waited for you. Monday, I went to work."

He moved to the bookshelves. Parenting books and children's books filled the two lower shelves. Pulling out one, he flipped through it. "No one would make eye contact with me. I was fired with a yellow Post-it note. I tried contacting your father. He told me that you'd be filing for divorce."

Book back in place, he braced his hand on the middle shelf and dropped his head. "I don't know if he told you about our conversation."

"No." She had begged her father to let her know what was going on, but he said it was all fine. "He told me that you wanted a divorce."

He made a strangling sound, as if someone were choking him. His spine stiffened, and his jaw went stone hard. Stomping across the room, he threw his long body into the other wicker chair and tilted his head back. "I told him I'd go to counseling. I begged him with everything I had to let me talk to you just once."

She gasped, her intertwined fingers pressed against her mouth. He was such a proud man. His pride wouldn't have ever allowed... "Oh, Elijah."

"I promised to stop drinking, but he rightfully reminded me that I'd said that before." He leaned forward, elbows braced on his knees. "He was right. But I still held out hope that you'd come back. You had always come back. I mean, your shampoo was in the bathroom."

Both hands went to his hair. "I went to their house to see you, but they put a restraining order against me."

He shot up like a jack-in-the-box unlatched. There was a hard crease between his eyes. "Did they know you were pregnant? That night, did they know?"

She couldn't say the words, but her silence

was enough. The distress in his eyes at that realization hit her hard.

A depth of grief she had never seen filled his eyes. "That whole time I was pleading to speak with you, they knew. They knew I was going to be a father." He pressed his palms against his eye sockets.

Her heart hurt for all the lost moments, but she needed to focus on the future, on what they could be together going forward.

He dragged his hands down his face, then paced. "They were trying to protect you. I get it. Just like I'd protect Rosemarie. Like I protected Gabby and eventually my sister." He closed his eyes and a deep painful groan came from his throat. "My daughter and wife had to be hidden from me."

"Elijah, they went too far." Standing, she cupped his face. "Have you been sober since the night I left?"

He shook his head, as if confused. "No. I was determined to be sober for you so that when you came back you'd see I could be a good husband. I went to my first AA meeting. A few weeks went by and still no word from you, then the restraining orders and the divorce papers arrived. I lost it. I didn't know how to deal with all the emotions, so I fell right back into old habits." He sat on the sofa with his elbows on his knees, and he watched her.

Sorting through all this new information was putting pressure on her head. "Right before I signed the divorce papers, I asked my parents to let me see you. They said you were worse than the last time I saw you. Were they telling me the truth?"

He dropped his head, his long fingers interlocked behind his head.

"Elijah? How long were you…"

"I don't remember anything about the week after I signed the papers." He still hadn't raised his head.

Was she hearing him, right? "One week? And you've been clean ever since?"

He nodded.

He'd been sober when their daughter was born and during most of her pregnancy. "What changed?"

"Xavier. Basically, he told me I had a choice to make. I could wallow in self-pity and have a miserable life and prove the Judge and your mother right. Or I could turn it all over to God and figure out my purpose. He said if I wanted to be like our fathers, I was on the right track."

She sat beside him. "Oh, Elijah. I know how much you respected your cousin's opinion."

He nodded. "He was right, as usual. I miss him so much."

Putting her fingers under his chin, she lifted his face to hers. "Even through losing him and finding you have a daughter you've stayed sober. You're so strong. He'd be so proud of you."

Moisture shimmered in his eyes. "Not me. God is my strength."

She didn't bother to point out that trusting God was what made him strong. But her gut told her it was time to change the subject. Or maybe her heart couldn't take any more arrows. "How'd you become a successful businessman in such a short time? You've impressed my father."

One dark eyebrow went up. "That heart attack must have affected the Judge's brain."

She laughed. "Maybe he sees the world a little clearer now." Leaning back to give him room, she tried to look relaxed. "So how did Saltwater Cowboys happen?"

"I couldn't get a job. I even went to my uncle, but he refused to let me on the ranch. I started working odd jobs on the pier. I'd bus tables at the restaurants, clean out the boats, whatever anyone would let me do. I started going out on the fishing boats more. That's where I met Miguel. He had business experience. I had grown up here, on the water. We make a good team."

He popped his knuckles. "Before I knew it, a year had gone by without a drink, and I realized I liked life better without the haze of alcohol. I started taking AA seriously. Xavier had one boat, so we went to him with our plan. I was able to use our house as collateral."

A heavy sigh escaped his lungs, and he fell back against the sofa. "One of the hardest periods of my recovery was letting go of you. In order to heal and move on from the past, I had to give up on the idea of you and me together."

His gaze roamed the living room and kitchen. He gave her a sad grin. "I'm pretty sure there's a part of me that tucked you away and held on."

She nodded. "A part of me stayed with you. My parents knew. That's why they fought so hard to keep you out of my life."

The sadness that always hovered in the edges of his eyes swallowed them. Putting a pillow on her lap, she studied his face.

"You had a part of me with you," he whispered.

"Yes. She was my strength when I was at my lowest. When I look at her, I see the best of you and me. I'm so sorry my parents kept—"

"Don't." His large hands covered hers on

the pillow. "I told you no more apologizing for protecting our daughter."

"I went through counseling, too. In one of the group sessions, I was asked if I would do it again. Would I marry you if it had to play out the same way? I said yes without hesitation. I would say yes, every single time."

He nodded. "Because of Rosemarie."

"She's one reason, but also because of you." She sat back and smiled. "Loving you was a great adventure. When you were sober, it was the greatest joy of my life. You taught me to enjoy the little things in life and to not always play by the rules. Like eating the center of the brownie first. Without the alcohol, you're the greatest man I know."

He made a rude noise. "Your father is the Judge. *The Judge*. That's what everyone says, with respect and honor. Sweetheart, there is no way—"

She pressed her fingertip against his lips. "Don't argue with me. My father is a great man and so are you. The real you. Not the man trying to be someone he's not. You're not my father. You're your own man, and I think you've found him."

He took her hand in his and kissed her palm, then her knuckles. For a moment she couldn't breathe, but then he dropped her hand and sat back. "But I also broke your heart."

"Yes. It was the biggest heartbreak of my life. But I grew up and wove my heart back together. It's stronger than ever. We can do the same thing. We can weave our broken life back together and be unbreakable."

"What do you mean, 'we'?" He narrowed his gaze, distrust written all over his face.

Excitement bubbled through her limbs. She was going to do it, take the plunge. "So much time was lost, time we can't get back. I want to come home."

"You're moving back to Texas?" He looked down, nodding. "Austin's not that far."

"Not Austin. Here."

His eyebrows scrunched, making hard lines in his forehead. "Port Del Mar? That's not a good idea."

"This is what I wanted to talk to you about." Leg tucked under her, she shifted to face him. "We're both in a better place now." She took his hand. Willing him to understand.

"You taught me to take chances. You showed me there was more life beyond the books and my parents." She grinned. "Don't get me wrong, I love my parents, but they kept me in a tight little box. You opened the world up to me in a way I would have never experienced it."

"Your parents had good reasons to protect you. Just like you should protect Rosemarie. She'll be exposed to the rumors about my family."

"We'll teach her the truth and how hurtful gossip is. You have nothing to be ashamed of." With a nervous laugh, she shook her head. "We can do that together. I want Rosie to grow up here. With time maybe we can even reclaim our dream of having a family."

Horror filled his face. "Jazmine, you can't be serious." He yanked his hands out of her grasp and stood.

"I'm so proud of everything you've accomplished. I should have come back sooner."

His jaw dropped and all the color left his face. "No." He stood and moved behind the kitchen counter.

She was offering him everything, and he was walking away. She didn't understand. Her brain scrambled for a way to make him see that this was what they both needed. Her nails cut into her palms. She would not cry. He just didn't understand.

She tried to make eye contact, but he turned away.

He stared out the window. "We have a plan. It's a good plan for everyone. I'll visit Denver during the year, and on holidays and in summer you'll come here with her."

"But what if I want more?" Each word had to be pushed past the sand in her throat.

"I have no more to offer."

"I'm stronger now. I know what I want. I… We can get it right this time." She followed him, needing him to understand.

His forehead was deeply creased. "And if we don't? You were never the problem in our relationship, you understand that, right?"

"I have accountability in this, too." She circled her arms around her waist. "I expected you to know what I was thinking and feeling. Instead of dealing with the real issues, I ran and hid. We've learned so much, and both of us are stronger in our faith."

She moved around the counter and put her hand on top of his, not letting him get away this time. "You were my world. I thought we would just love each other enough and the problems would go away. I loved you so much. We could have that again."

He pulled away. "I destroyed your world."

"You won't do that again. I won't let you." The lopsided cup caught her eye. Picking it up, she traced the uneven surface. "This cup isn't perfect, but our daughter made it with perfect love. Just like that mirror, we can build a new world. A better world. A world that can survive the storm."

"I don't want you or Rosemarie anywhere near me if that storm hits again. It's never far. If you're in Denver with her, you'll be safe."

"That's what you want? For me and Rosemarie to be over a thousand miles from you?"

He wouldn't look at her. "I can be a good weekend dad. I didn't cut it as an everyday husband." He started pacing. "You want me to pull out my family history? Your parents had it right. You and Rosemarie need to be as far away from the De La Rosa family as possible."

"She is a De La Rosa," she whispered. She wanted to grab him and make him face her, stare into her eyes until he understood that he deserved to be loved. "Elijah, please."

"No. You made sure she was a Daniels. Which might be best in the long run. The De La Rosa legacy will not be hers."

"You can't let Frank define who you are."

"I'm not, but some things are facts."

"I don't believe it."

He dropped his shoulders, as if the fight had left his body. He rubbed his fingers hard against his forehead.

She stood on the edge, waiting for him to join her. Needing him to join her. Everything she ever dreamed of was in front of her if he would only take her hand.

Elijah forced himself to step away from her. It would be too easy to grab the hand she offered and hang on. But he knew better. Her eyes sparkled with excitement. He didn't want to be the one who took that away. Not again.

"You really want her to grow up in a town where she'll be known as one of those De La Rosas? And don't you dare lie to me. You wouldn't even give her my name, and you were all the way in Denver."

"I regret that. You and your cousins have changed the legacy of your family name. I'm proud of you and I want Rosemarie to see that, to be a part of your life, here in Port Del Mar."

Loser. Worthless. Drunk. He didn't want his daughter to hear those words about him. He couldn't breathe. Turning sharply on his heels, he went through the double doors to the back deck. The waves crashed against the shore.

He felt her hand on the center of his back, circling in a soothing motion. He closed his eyes. Longing for everything he lost swirled in his head. The desire to give in. To tell her yes.

Her touch was as soft as gentle waves. "Some of the best moments of my life happened right here. We could have the future we dreamed of if you have the faith."

Gently, he stepped back, disconnecting them. Turning, he held her arm, palm up. His fingers traced the jagged scar that sliced her palm. "I did this to you."

"You didn't cause my injury."

His head tilted back. He closed his eyes. "I should have been your safe place."

"We were young and made mistakes."

"Sometimes letting go and moving on is the best second chance we can hope for."

"No. You apologized, right? Everything about your life since I left shows you meant it. You don't think you deserve to be happy."

Blinking did not ease the burn behind his eyes. How did he answer that? His jaw locked.

"You don't, do you?"

He felt raw. It was like she was gouging his chest, exposing all his weakness. "I'm happy with my life. What I don't deserve is your trust. I'm toxic. I live one day at a time. I can't promise you a future. I can't promise that in one month or ten years I'll be the man I am today."

He ran his hand through his hair to stop himself from grabbing her. "I'm one drink away from being Ben, drunk in the parking lot fighting with a friend who's trying to help me."

"I'm not the same pushover. We belong together. Our daughter deserves to grow up in the home we built. You're my husband. In my heart you always have been, even after I signed the papers." Her gaze scorched him. "Elijah, could you grow to love me again?" Fear and doubt etched each word.

His face tightened. *I love you so much. I've loved you forever.* The words fought to get past his lips, but they wouldn't budge. They lodged in his throat. He needed them to stay buried.

"The question was never whether I loved you. Do I love you enough to walk away, to protect you? I'm one drink away from being the man that chased you away. He's still inside me. Lurking."

"God has you."

"Jazmine, I'm an alcoholic. My life happens one day at a time. That's all I have. All I can offer. It's not good enough."

Her lips parted.

"There is no cure for what I have. We can't do this to Rosemarie." Tears were running down his face, but he was powerless to stop them. "If I go down again, I'm not pulling you with me. Don't trust me."

"I trust God."

An exasperated huff of air escaped his lungs. "Stop being stubborn." He took a deep breath, calming himself, then lowered his voice. "I'm doing this for you. What if our love isn't stronger than the addiction?" He shook his head. "I can't risk losing control and her seeing that side of me."

"Do you regret marrying me?" The hard edge of her voice softened.

He couldn't answer that. She was his life. The world was a better place with her in it. He was a better man because she was in his world. He swallowed, not blinking, as their eyes stayed locked.

"Okay." Head down, she smoothed the pretty pink skirt that floated around her legs. She had been so innocent when he first met her.

"You deserve better than me." He needed her to get that it was about saving her, not hurting her. "So does our daughter, but she's stuck with me as her father. I'll do the best I can, but I can't promise anything long-term."

Her breath hitched, and her body stiffened. "You're a coward." It was a harsh whisper between clenched teeth.

He was doing this for his family. He was going to be a man of courage for the first time in his life. "If that's what it takes to keep you both safe, then I guess I'm a coward. Go back to Denver, Jazz."

Back straight, she lifted her chin. Her eyes searched his face and her mouth opened, as if she had more to say. He braced himself. He couldn't be weak now.

"It's over, Jazmine. Let me go."

She swung around and walked out the door. This time, she wouldn't be coming back. The urge to yell at her, to beg her to keep fight for him, hit him like a tidal wave taking him under. Pulling everything out, leaving him hollow.

The door clicked shut behind her, and he fell to his knees and prayed. Tears fell hard. He wanted to reach inside and rip his heart out. He just needed to stop the pain. His elbows hit the ground, and he buried his fingers in his hair. "Please God. You're my strength." With her light gone, the darkness threatened to overtake him. This time he wouldn't let it.

He scoured his mind for a verse. John 12:46. "'I am come a light into the world, that whosoever believeth on me should not abide in darkness. I am come a light into the world, that whosoever believeth on me should not abide in darkness.'"

On the floor, he repeated the verse over and over again.

Chapter Fifteen

The moon looked as if it hung right above her parents' house. Pulling into the shadow of the tall, three-story home, Jazmine parked her car. She rested her head against the steering wheel and sobbed. She had been able to hold the worst of it back as she drove, but she was safe in her parents' driveway now.

A tap on the window caused her to jump right along with her heart. Her mother stood in the dark. Hand on her chest, Jazmine opened the door. "What are you doing? You scared me half to death."

"I'm sorry, pumpkin." Without another word, Azalea pulled her grown daughter into her arms and rocked her like a child.

After a few minutes of crying until her throat and ribs hurt, she sat back and wiped at her face. "Mom, what are you doing out here?"

"I was waiting for you on the balcony, but when you didn't get out of the car I got worried." Tucking a loose curl behind Jazmine's ear, Azalea laid her forehead against her daughter's. "It didn't go the way you wanted? You were gone a long time."

"No." Jazmine stepped back and rubbed the back of her hand across her face. A stupid sob escaped.

Her mother took her by the hand and pulled her to the back door. "Let's go sit on the balcony. I have lemonade and brownies waiting for you."

The crying started all over.

Once on the top balcony, she settled in and allowed her mother to pamper her. Jazmine noticed the Bible open on the table. "What have you been reading?"

"My Bible study group has been discussing Romans. This week, Romans 5:8 was part of our reading, and it stuck with me. I was praying over it while you were gone."

Jazmine leaned back in the rocker and sipped her drink, trying to let the stress float past her. "What does it say?"

"'But God commendeth his love toward us, in that, while we were yet sinners, Christ died for us.'"

The corner of her mouth curled. "You've concluded that God loves Elijah."

"Oh, it's much more personal than that. God loves me despite my own sin, yet I sit here judging Elijah for actions from the past. What does the last six years tell me about him? It's the plank in my eye while I point out your splinter. Don't get me wrong. Getting you out that night? I would do it again. But the following months should have been handled differently. He has to hate us, but he's been very patient."

"We talked about that tonight. He understands why you hid us. He did the same for his family. Part of his healing has involved letting go of the past and the anger and taking responsibility for his actions."

Her mother sighed. "So, why the tears?"

Her throat burned. If she spoke, the tears would start all over again.

Azalea slid into the large rocker next to her. "What happened?"

"He doesn't want us to be close."

Warmth surrounded her as her mother pulled her into her arms. The crying started all over again. When the sobs finally subsided, she leaned back, focusing on the stars so far away.

"Tuesday, we'll be leaving for Denver." With a slight turn of her head, she looked at her mother and gave her the best smile she could manage. "The message was loud and clear. Not only is there no future for us as a family, he thinks we should go back to Denver. As far from him as possible. That should reassure you."

Azalea didn't let go of Jazmine's hands. "No, baby. All I ever wanted was for you to be happy. I thought you were happy in Denver, but after watching you the last few weeks, I realize you were just surviving. You're a great mother, but I think a part of you was missing. Maybe it's time for you to come back."

Jazmine frowned. "Rosemarie and I are fine in Denver. She'll get to see her father every other weekend and spend summers with her grandparents."

Azalea put her arm around her daughter, resting her chin on the top of Jazmine's head. "I know I've tried everything in my power to keep you from Elijah. But some things are in God's hands. These last few weeks there's been a joy in you I haven't seen in years. I think you belong here, with Elijah."

"Mom?" She pulled back and looked at her mother, stunned. "What have you done with my mother?" Sighing, she shook her head and rested on her mother's shoulder. "You might have changed your opinion, but it doesn't matter. He doesn't want me in his life."

"That man loves you. He always has. I've seen how he treats Rosemarie. He's a good father. If I truly believe that God can change people, then I believe the evidence in Elijah's life. Not just this summer, but what he's done since you left. You wanted to fight for him after that first weekend, but you were so hurt and lost. It was easy for us to take care of everything and send you away. Are you strong enough to fight for him now?"

Fresh tears made their way up from the bottom of her heart. "I don't know."

"He tried everything short of breaking down our door to get to you, and that was before he knew about Rosemarie."

Jazmine sat up. "It's true? You and Daddy lied to me." She closed her eyes. The betrayal hit hard. She had based so many decisions on the lies her parents had told her. "You told me he wanted the divorce. When I asked how he was doing, you said his drinking was worse."

"It was." The words were sharp and defensive. Azalea dropped her head. "The time I went…" She looked back up at Jazmine, her eyes softer, regret deep. "It was the week after he signed the papers. I went to the house and, well, it wasn't pleasant. That was the last time

I saw him in that condition or heard about him drinking."

"He told me he had one setback when he realized I wasn't coming home."

Her mother took her hands in hers, and Jazmine saw tears in her eyes. "Oh sweetheart, I'm so sorry. We just wanted to protect you. It's not an excuse, but I didn't know what else to do. I was so afraid I'd lose you. I'd do anything to keep you safe. We went too far."

Pulling away, Jazmine stood and went to the railing. The moon hung low in the night sky, the reflection dancing on the waves. "You know he said that? He said he understood why you did what you did. He's trying to protect us." She turned back to her mother. "From him." The tears started falling again.

Coming to her side, Azalea wrapped an arm around her. "You're a good mother. You'd never put Rosie at risk. He's proving to be a good father. If you think the best place for you both is with him, I'll support you."

"Are you sure?"

Her mother's gentle hand on her cheek took her back to childhood. "In my need to control, you might not notice this, but I do trust you. I also see the world a little differently these days." She kissed her temple. "I almost lost your father. I'm working on trusting God more.

That's not easy for me. Elijah is surrounded by the good choices he's made since you left. You need to stay true to your heart. God has you, follow Him."

"It's that easy?"

"Yes and no. Nothing of true value is easy." Her mother cupped Jazmine's face. "You're strong, my beautiful daughter. God will show you the way. And I'll support you."

Did she know the right thing to do for all of them? Jazmine looked at the time. Elijah would be here bright and early to take them fishing. He didn't trust himself, and she had only reinforced that by not allowing him to be responsible for Rosemarie.

She needed to prove to both that he was trustworthy.

"Mommy! Mommy! Wake up."

Jazmine groaned at the weight bouncing on her bed. Forcing one eye open, she peered at the time. It was almost five o'clock. Why was Rosie…? She shot up. "Your father!"

With all the drama last night, she'd forgotten to make sure her alarm was set. She rubbed her face.

"Daddy said to be ready by five. You're not ready."

Blinking her eyes, she focused on her daughter. Rosemarie was wearing a Painted Dolphin T-shirt, jeans, and the pink and purple waders Elijah had bought her. And a purple tutu. Oh, to be five and wear whatever struck your mood.

The tutu matched her new fishing pole. She was even wearing Jazmine's oversize hat.

"What do you think about making this a day with your dad and cousins, a De La Rosa trip?" She needed to prove to Elijah that she did trust him. Plus, spending all day with him in the confines of a boat might prove too much for her right now. Her emotions were still raw. And she had a great deal of praying to do.

"But you're coming. You don't want to fish?"

"It's not really my thing. Anyway, I thought you might like a little time alone with your father."

Rosie plopped onto the bed. "We could talk about you." She giggled.

Before she could ask what, they would talk about, there was a knock on the door.

"He's here! Mommy, you're still in your pajamas."

Her pajamas consisted of an oversize Jim's Pier T-shirt and yoga pants. Slipping out of bed, she threw her robe on. "Go get your fishing pole and backpack."

Then she stumbled down the steps, trying to push her hair into some sort of civilized shape.

Opening the door, she came face-to-face with the same Painted Dolphin logo that Rosemarie had picked out to wear. Elijah's fit a little tighter, stretching across broad shoulders. Very broad shoulders.

She blinked a couple of times, trying to escape the sleep fog that clouded her thoughts. Moving her gaze up, she was trapped by her favorite set of eyes. This morning they seem to dance in between shades of gray and green.

She frowned. The look of hesitation and doubt she found in them hurt her heart. With a shake of her head, she glared at him. He had no right to be all sad. He was the one who had rejected her.

Last night she had gone to him, and he had turned her down. Why was he looking like the kicked puppy?

"Do I have the wrong day?" He glanced around, as if the date was written in the air.

"No."

"We're going fishing, right?"

"Yes." *Brilliant, Jazmine.* It seemed as if one word at a time was all her brain could manage.

His gaze dropped to her bare feet. "I wouldn't recommend going barefoot."

"Oh, I'm not going. I'm not feeling well, so I decided today you can take her without me."

He closed the distance between them and put the back of his hand on her forehead. "We can reschedule."

She stepped back. "No, no. I'm not that sick. Just didn't sleep well last night."

The crease in Elijah's brow deepened. He searched her eyes. What was he looking for?

"Just her and me? You're going to let me take her? Out on a boat?"

This should have happened so long ago. She covered her face with her oversize terry-cloth sleeve. She was not going to cry again. Forcing a smile, she nodded. "It's time."

"Jazmine, I'm sorry. I know last night wasn't what you had expected." He stuffed his hands in his back pockets, stretching his shoulders wider. "I'm so tired of letting you down. It seems it's all I ever do."

She took a step closer but made sure not to touch him. Yelling at him to be brave and take a chance with them, was not a viable option this morning. She had said all the words last night, and it hadn't made a difference.

He lowered his chin until their foreheads almost touched. "Please, don't look at me like that. This is the first time in my life I'm not taking the easy way out. I'm doing this for her. And you."

Rosemarie's excited footsteps bounced down the stairs, and they jumped apart. Their daughter hopped off the last step and ran to Elijah. He went down to her level and opened his arms.

Hugging her tight, he pretended to be knocked off balance. "You're so strong!"

"Careful, sweetheart. You're going to hit someone with that fishing pole."

Elijah laughed. "Here, let me take it. I have a special place for it in my truck."

"Will you keep it there, even when Mommy takes me back to Denver? We can still fish every week, right?"

"Rosie." She put a hand on her tiny shoulder. "We can't come back every week. It's too far away."

The child's body stiffened, and a hard scowl took over the sweet face. She took in a lungful of air. Jazmine had a feeling Elijah was about to get a firsthand experience of stubborn Rosemarie. "Then I don't want to go to Denver. My fishing pole won't be there or my horse or GiGi and Papa." She took a breath. "I want to stay with Daddy. I want to live on the boat."

Elijah took a step back.

He had been the one to say no, and now he

wasn't going to say a word. She gathered her daughter's wild curls and put them in a ponytail. "Sweetheart, we've talked about this, but if you want to throw a fit, you're more than welcome to go to your room. If you want to go fishing with your daddy, you need to put on a smile. We can talk about this later if you want to, but not right now. Do you want to go fishing or throw a fit in your room?"

"Fishing."

"Good." Jazmine looked at her ex-husband. He had the deer-stuck-in-the-headlights look. "Elijah, are you ready?"

Elijah looked a bit lost as Rosemarie stood, fishing pole in hand. Clearing his throat, he dropped to one knee in front of their daughter. "I'll be coming to visit at least once a month. We'll have a great time when I'm there. You can show me your school and all your friends. You miss them, right?"

Rosemarie scowled.

Jazmine wanted to explain to him that a five-year-old didn't have a good grasp of time and distance. But Elijah stood, and those beautiful lips kicked up on each end.

Her heart skipped. There was the carefree boy she had fallen in love with so long ago. He offered his hand to Rosie. "You want to go fishing, or what?"

Rosemarie took it, her scowl vanishing.

Elijah glanced at Jazmine, his face suddenly serious. "I'll have her back before noon."

She crossed her arms. "It's okay if you want to take her to lunch."

"That's seven hours. Without you or your parents."

"You've always been good at math." Serious again, Jazmine tilted her head. "I trust you with her."

He gave a solemn nod.

"Daddy, we're going to catch big fish, just like on the TV." Rosemarie pulled at him, moving to his truck.

Jazmine smiled. "Save some. We can have them for dinner tonight. Papa needs to eat more fish. And take pictures to show me."

"Okay! Love you, Mommy!" Rosie yelled over her shoulder, eager to go off with her father.

"I love you too, sweetheart." The urge to cry burned her eyes. Was she going to stay and fight, or was he right? Would it be best for their daughter to keep things as they were?

He paused. Turning away from Rosemarie, he studied her.

Did he know what she was thinking? "Elijah?"

His eyes looked teal right then. "Do you want to join us for lunch?"

She shook her head. "I wanted to go to Dad's doctor visit."

"Daddy! Hurry, so we can sneak up on the fish before they wake up."

The left side of his lips curled. "Duty calls."

Jazmine laughed. "She's always been a morning baby. Up early and ready to attack the day—or the fish. She's all your daughter this morning." She yawned. "Sorry."

He grinned. "We'll see you this afternoon. Go back to bed, princess."

Rosemarie bounced beside the truck, excited about her new adventure.

"Don't forget to make her wear a life jacket."

Elijah strapped Rosemarie into the backseat of his truck. He had a booster chair all ready. He saluted Jazmine and winked. "Yes, Mom."

She stood and watched them disappear.

Six years ago, she had run without looking back. She was so tired of running. She needed Elijah to see the future she saw when she looked at him. But if he didn't, why was she fighting him? Putting her family back together wasn't something she could do on her own; he needed to want it too.

Chapter Sixteen

Elijah sat back in the shade of the canopy as the boat headed to land. Rosemarie had crawled into his lap and was chatting away about the fish she'd caught.

He couldn't believe he had her all to himself. Jazmine had actually allowed him to take their daughter out into the Gulf. With the curiosity of a five-year-old, she had asked tons of questions about the boat, and it was obvious she had a love for being outdoors. He wanted to do this with her every weekend.

"Could I work on the boats with you, Daddy? Tío Miguel said I would be a great second mate." Rosemarie had picked up that Belle's girls called his best friend "Uncle" and had started doing it, too.

"You would make the most excellent second mate." But she was going to be in Denver. He closed his eyes and leaned his cheek on the top of her head.

Someone sat down next to him. Opening his eyes, he found his sister staring at him. She looked as if she was about to cry. Alarmed, he lifted his head. "What's wrong?" He glanced down at his daughter and discovered the reason the chatter had stopped.

Mouth hanging open as if she had stopped in midsentence, she was sound asleep, her cheek pressed against the purple life vest. Shifting so he could pull her closer, he glanced back at Belle. Her smile was back in place.

"Are you okay?" he asked. Everything in this moment was perfect. But if his sister needed him, they would deal with whatever had to be done.

"I'm fine. You're the one I'm worried about. Are they still going back to Denver?"

He nodded. If he put real words to what was going to happen, he might lose control of his emotions. His arms tightened around the little body in his lap, as if that simple action would keep her in his life.

"Have you thought about how you're going to feel with her living in another state?"

His jaw flexed, pushing down the words that wanted to escape. *Every moment.*

Belle tugged at the bottom of her T-shirt. "I'm sorry. Of course, you've thought about that."

"How did one little person become such an important part of my everyday life? I want her here, but that's not fair to her." The sway of the boat usually calmed him, but it wasn't working right now. He'd give anything to change his history. But his history was always going to be part of him.

Belle leaned in close and stroked back a wild curl. A sad smile pierced his heart, and she looked up at him. "Have you thought about asking her to stay? I've seen y'all together. You're a new man and she sees that."

Eyes closed, he tilted his head back against the side of the boat.

She didn't allow him to hide in silence. Gripping his arm tighter, she leaned in. "Ask her to stay."

Inhaling deeply, he shook his head. "Last night she came to the house to tell me that she wanted to stay in town. Give us a second chance."

Belle gasped, her eyes bright with excitement. "Oh, Elijah!" She covered her mouth, trying to stay quiet.

"I told her no."

Confusion replaced her excitement faster than he blinked. "What?"

"She wanted to see if we had a future as a real family." Great. Now his eyes were burning, and he didn't have a free arm to wipe his face.

"How can you tell her no? You can have everything you've worked for. Her, your daughter and your business. I don't understand how you could walk away."

"Here's the deal, Belle. That guy who made her worry and wait until the early hours of the morning, the one who tore up our house? He still lives in me. He's part of me and always will be. She wants a commitment to a future that I can't give her. I can't do forever. I can't do six months. I have to live day by day. That's all I have to offer her."

"That's not true." Belle stood, her arms tight across her chest. She turned to him, about to say something, when Miguel came down the ladder.

He looked from one to the other. "What's going on?"

"Mr. Brilliant over here turned down the best offer he's ever going to get."

Miguel's brows went up. "Jazmine?"

"Yes, Jazmine. She wants to stay to give them another chance. He sent her away. *Terco*." She tapped the side of his head.

"I might be stubborn, but that doesn't mean I'm wrong."

"Why would you reject her?" He looked at Belle.

She twirled her finger next to her head. *"Loco."*

"Shh. Don't wake her up." Elijah wanted out of this conversation. "You're both messing with my live-in-the-moment moment. Go away."

"Listen." Miguel ignored him and sat on the opposite chair. "You have every reason to say yes to her. To them. To this moment." He indicated the child innocently sleeping in Elijah's arms. "Why are you punishing yourself?"

Elijah glared at Belle. "Did you tell him to say that?"

She rolled her eyes. "No one has to tell anyone to say that. We all see it."

The walls were closing in on him. Breathing became harder. "I'm always one drink away, Belle. One drink away from being Uncle Frank."

"No. Even at your worst, you couldn't be him. It's not in you."

"I don't think there's any way to get through that thick *cabeza*." Miguel sighed. "I came down to take your daughter to see a pod of dolphins. They're ahead of the boat. We have a great view from the upper deck. Cassie and Lucy are up there with Carlos."

Elijah gently shook Rosemarie. "Hey, sweetheart, you want to see a family of dolphins?"

She was on her feet and looking around. "Where?"

Miguel held out his hand. "One thing your Tío Miguel can do better than anyone else is find dolphins. Want to see them?"

She grabbed his hand and nodded. "Can I, Daddy?"

"Of course, you can. It's why we're out here."

Belle moved closer to her. "We'll be up in a minute."

With a smile and a nod, they were gone.

He shook his head. "There's nothing else to say. I'm not going to let the woman I love and my daughter ever live in a house with the monster I could become."

"You never drove drunk. You never physically harmed her."

"Woo-hoo!" He twirled his fingers in the air. "Give me the husband of the year award." His gaze went to the scar along the left side of her forehead, near her eye.

She got right in his face. "Don't go there. You are nothing like either one of those men."

"Just because the scars I gave her are all inside doesn't make it better. You know as well as I do that emotional injuries can be more damaging than the ones everyone can see." His finger traced her jagged scar.

His sister wrapped her fingers around his hand. "Even at your worst, you never hurt someone weaker than you. Not even verbally. Without you, I wouldn't have survived. I'm so tired of watching you punish yourself. You asked for forgiveness. God forgives you, Jazmine has forgiven you, so why can't you forgive yourself?"

"How can they forgive me?" That was the question that had rattled around in his head from the start. The question he shouldn't ask if his faith was good enough. "I shouldn't doubt God's word, but how can forgiveness be so easy? It doesn't make sense."

"That's what faith's all about. Believing what doesn't make sense in this world. It's God's kingdom. God's love. It's way beyond our feeble understanding. You have a gift that has been beautifully wrapped. Take it and treasure it."

He dropped his head. "I can't."

"Have you stopped loving her?"

"Loving her isn't the problem. I've always loved her. Even when I moved on from the divorce, I couldn't think of dating someone else."

He looked out into the afternoon sky. "She's it for me, but I can't risk—"

"Stop right there, Elijah Gilbert De La Rosa. You love her. She loves you. Why are you wasting time being such an idiot?"

"Hello. Alcoholic." He held his arms out wide and pointed to himself. "And I've seen guys sober for years lose it all in one glass. When they fall off, they tend to fall off really hard."

"So, you're cutting her and your daughter out of your life. Too bad, so sad, Rosemarie doesn't get a father." Belle clenched her teeth and paced. "I know you think you're doing the heroic thing, but you're denying them your love as much as you're denying yourself theirs. You're letting fear win."

"I'm protecting her. I want her in my life. But if she's in town, people will tell her what a loser her father is. A drunk. If they're in Denver, she won't be hurt if I fall."

Stopping, Belle turned and stared at him, eyes wide, mouth open.

He rolled his eyes. "Close your mouth, you're letting flies in."

With a thump, she flopped into the chair next to him. "You really believe if you fall off the wagon, living in Denver will save her feelings? You're her daddy. This little girl loves you. No matter where she lives, what you do will affect her."

Wetness hovered on her lashes. His gut curled. Why was he always making the women he loved cry?

She reached over and gently touched his cheek. "She loves you, and you'll be the best dad because you'll wake up every morning and promise her another day. You'll commit to her one day at a time, every single day. That's how you got sober. The same way you built your business. Look at what you've accomplished, one day at a time."

Something inside him shifted, hard. He couldn't let that happen. He had to keep it there, because if he… He popped his knuckles. "What if I lose my sobriety?"

"You get up and you fix it. You're not protecting her by sending her away. Listen to me." She grabbed his ear and forced him to look at her. "It doesn't matter how far away you send her. If you fall, it's going to hurt her. Jazmine knows what she's doing. She said she loves you, and she wants to commit to a future with you. Trust her and love her and lean on God to take care of the rest. Can you picture a life without her?"

No. "I can, but not one I want to live."

"Do you trust God?"

Oh, that was harder. "With her heart? It's not God I don't trust. It's me."

"Then you've already hurt her. You're only giving her little parts of you. That's never going to be good enough. Your daughter and your wife need all of you. The good, the bad and the imperfect. You're a good man, and they deserve all of your love."

Could he say yes to Jazmine? He shook his head. "I can't."

"You won't."

He sighed. "I have a few days left with my daughter. I'm going to watch dolphins and do anything else she wants." He moved to the steps, then stopped in front of her. His knuckle traced the edge of her scar. "You didn't do anything to deserve this, Belle. If anyone deserves to be fully loved, it's you."

"We don't always get what we deserve. I've got everything I need—my girls, a family I can count on, a business I love and God. What else do I need? A man? No, thanks. Anyway, who would I date? All the men around here know my past. Jazmine knows us. She knows you, all of you, and she still believes in you. Think about that. Now, go be with your daughter."

He nodded and swung around, jumping up the ladder. His stomach tightened, but he couldn't focus on the days ahead. Right now he had Rosemarie, and he wanted her to have good memories of her father.

The kind to let her know he loved her even if he falls.

His sister was right. Giving her the childhood he never had could happen one day at a time.

Each morning he could wake up and promise to love them through the day. Day that could make up years.

Was it too late? Had he pushed Jazmine past the point of forgiving him ever again?

Chapter Seventeen

The sun was peeking over the water as he drove to the three-story beach home. To Jazmine. He was not going to let them get on that plane tomorrow without laying his heart on the line like she had done for him. He had been a coward that night.

Stepping out of his truck, Elijah looked to the top of the three-story beach house. He closed his eyes. *Please, God, give me the words and the strength I need to do this work.* For the last few days, he had gone back and forth on and circled every word his sister had said.

Letting Jazmine go had not been for the good of her and their daughter.

He could give her one day, each day. Together they could watch the sun rise and make a new vow each morning to love one another.

The same as he vowed to God each morning to turn his problem over to him.

He stood at the door, wiping his hands over his jeans. Had he waited too long?

Before he knocked, the front door opened. "Elijah?"

Jazmine's mother stood on the threshold.

"Yes, ma'am."

She stepped farther out and closed the door behind her. "They're not here."

All the blood drained from his body, and his head went blank. They couldn't be gone. "No. It's too early."

"She got a call yesterday. There was an emergency at work, and they asked her to come back. They left on the next flight out. Didn't she call you?"

"I had a missed call from her and a message she wanted to talk, but…" She hadn't want to tell him over the phone. "I had Lane cover my charter today and came over to talk." It seemed she had decided to move on just like he told her. What did he do now?

He looked Azalea in the eye. "I love her. I love them both."

"I know."

"You also know I don't deserve her." He stood before her with his hat in his hands.

"My daughter loves you. She never stopped.

I don't want to see her hurt, and I trust you want the same. That's what I've seen this summer, anyway. In God I trust. If you do the same, this will be good for everyone."

There was a new lightness in his chest. "I won't take her for granted. I need to talk with her."

"Wait here a moment." She wasn't gone long and when she returned, she handed him a box.

"A ring box?"

"It's her great-grandmother's. It has an incredible love story attached to it. The world didn't think they belonged together, but they proved everyone wrong by loving each other for over fifty years and filling their days with happiness." She picked up his hand and wrapped his fingers around the box.

"You're giving it to me?" He had no clue how to react, what to say.

"I'm not saying you should give this to her right now. You probably have a few things to talk about, but I can't imagine anyone else giving this to her. She asked for it the first time you got married. I didn't think you were right for her, so I refused to let her have it. Of course, that didn't stop her from marrying you."

Tears gathered in her long eyelashes. His own chest felt as though a vise grip was squeezing his ribs. "We rushed the first time. It was a mistake."

"No. The alcohol was the mistake, not the marriage. You told Jazmine it was fear that led you to drinking. That's the reason you lost her." Azalea placed her hand on his shoulder. "I've had my own recent lesson. Fear is a lie you believe. That lie will mess up your future."

"Being an alcoholic is not a lie."

"You didn't beat the odds because of luck, but by faith. Leaning on God, you've fought hard to stay sober. The man standing at my door decided he wanted to own the largest fleet of boats in Port Del Mar, and he made it happen."

She clasped her hands in front of her and took a moment to search his eyes, her gaze firm and intense. "You wanted a real relationship with your daughter, and despite my best efforts—" a chuckle softened her words "—you're not just her biological father, you're the daddy she loves. You even won over a mother-in-law who was letting bitterness blind her. With each goal set, you've not only achieved, you've exceeded."

"I didn't do it alone."

"No. None of us survive this life by going it alone."

Elijah looked down. A few more arrows of doubt hit him.

"She's seen you at your worst and knows you at your best. She's willing to put her trust in God that together you'll make the family she has always wanted."

Raising his head, Elijah took a deep breath and rolled his shoulders. "I think God's been trying to talk to me. And, as usual, I've been stubbornly ignoring Him."

"God's good. He won't give up on you. And I don't think she will, either." Sincerity softened Azalea's dark brown eyes.

"I'm starting to see that." God had put so many people in his life who had helped him find the right path. "I keep hearing Jazz, Miguel, my sister, all telling me the same thing. God might be bringing in the big guns to pop me on the back of the head."

"Me?" Her eyes twinkled.

Elijah nodded.

"I hope you're listening."

"You think I should go to Denver?"

She rolled her eyes. "Why are you still standing here?"

With the tip of her finger, Azalea patted the corner of her eye. "Go get her. Love them like they're the most precious things in your life."

"They are." Certainty pulled every nerve

taut. On impulse, he hugged her. "I'll always protect them, even if it's from me."

She nodded against his shoulder and patted his back. "I know."

He was ready to lay it all out there. As he pulled out of the drive, plans started forming in his head. He would do whatever it took to prove to her that he was worth the risk. Would it be groveling or a big gesture? Maybe a little of both.

Hopefully, she still wanted him.

Chapter Eighteen

Jazmine looked around the decorated ballroom covered in soothing ocean blue. There was that little something extra missing for the fund-raiser, but it could have been much worse. The event had been on the edge of disaster. Her boss had called her when the man who had covered her position left without notice and they discovered he had done next to nothing with the plans she had left him.

"Ms. Daniels." One of the interns rushed in with a large box. She was followed by two others carrying the same kind of box.

The use of her maiden name tugged at her heart, which was ridiculous. Elijah had made it clear he wanted to move on. So three days ago she had returned to Denver, and for her daughter's sake she was going to have to get over this deep sense of loss. She was not part of the De La Rosa family. But her daughter was. She needed to talk to Rosie about adding Elijah's name to hers.

Elijah. She blinked back unwanted tears. They had been playing phone tag, but not actually saying anything in their messages. Irritated with herself, she focused on Claire's excited face.

"These were just delivered to you. I think they're exactly what you were looking for to finish off the tables. I love the wooden starfish. You were holding back on us. There have to be over three hundred."

Paul, the newest intern, picked one up. "They each have a tag that reads, 'One at a time.'"

"I didn't order these." She looked on the box for any clues. They were from a gift shop in Del Port Mar. Oh, no. The stupid tears were trying to escape again. She needed to make herself busy.

Claire pulled more starfish out of the boxes and arranged them on the table. "These will be perfect gifts to the donors. Let's scatter them on the tabletops."

Not understanding how this was happening, Jazmine lifted one out of the box, a light turquoise starfish. "Do you know the story?"

Paul shook his head.

Claire laid a couple on another table. "It's about the boy walking along the beach?"

Jazmine nodded. "Yes. He was throwing the stranded starfish back into the ocean to save their lives. When an older man laughed at him and said there were too many for him to make a difference, he gently put another on back into the ocean then smiled and said—"

Someone cut her off by clearing his throat. She turned expecting her boss but froze in place when she saw Elijah. "He said, 'I made a difference to that one.' One at a time."

In a well-cut suit, he stood with his hands clasped in front of him. Her mind went blank.

"Hi, Jazz." He walked across the room.

"What are you doing here?" Then it hit her square in the center of her head. "Rosie. I'm sorry about taking off like that I tried calling but—"

This time he cut her off with his thumb on her bottom lip. "I know." He glanced over her shoulder.

"Um. Sorry. Claire, Paul and Monica are interns." She waved in Elijah's direction. "This is Elijah De La Rosa. He's Rosie's father."

There was a chorus of "ohs." Claire had a starfish in her hand. "Did you send these? There's a bunch."

He grinned. "Yes. Three hundred and sixty-five to be exact." His gaze found Jazmine again. "One for each day of the year. It's been pointed out to me by several people that I've accomplished some pretty good stuff with my one day at a time philosophy."

He had done more than some good stuff, but she couldn't seem to find any words.

Leaning in, his lips were so close to her ear that she could feel his breath. "Is there somewhere we can talk?"

"My office." She nodded, then gave final instructions to the interns before taking him to her private office. Closing the door, she leaned against it for support. "I can't believe you're here."

One hip on her desk, he crossed his arms. "I messed up, Jazz. You thought we had a future in Port D and I...well, I was stupid and scared." He stood and stalked toward her. "Tell me what's going on in that brilliant mind of yours."

She couldn't comprehend this man. Words tried to organize themselves in her head, but before she could get them out into the air between them, he closed in. Taking all her personal space.

Sharing space with him was something she had always loved. His scent comforted her in ways nothing else ever could.

He leaned in and pressed his mouth to hers, cutting off any words. The feel, taste and scent of Elijah De La Rosa consumed her.

At this moment he was the only thing in her world. She liked her world.

She never wanted to leave this world.

His hands cupped her face and she leaned deeper into his warmth. But then cool air touched her lips as he pulled back.

She tried to follow, but he held her in place. With his hands still holding her, he put space between them. Her hands went to his wrists, making sure they kept contact. The word *no* fought its way up her throat, but she bit it back and waited.

His fingers gently dug into her hair. "I got ahead of myself. Everything I said about letting you go and moving on was a lie."

"What do you want from me? You told me to return to Denver, and I did. You send me hundreds of starfish after you gave me a hundred reasons why I shouldn't stay in Port Del Mar. You come in here and kiss me like you have a right to. You're in a suit. And I don't—"

One corner of his mouth curled up.

She frowned at him. "What's so funny?"

"You get really wordy when you're nervous." He moved in again, pressing his forehead to hers. "Are you done?"

"I don't know."

He chuckled. "While you're thinking of other things to tell me, I have something I need to say to you."

His face was so close she could see all the beautiful colors that made up his eyes. The ring around his irises was an indigo blue. That was new.

He cleared his throat. "I went to your parents' place to tell you something I should have said at our house the other night when you offered me everything I ever dreamed of. Things I didn't think I deserved. This morning, Romans 11:29 was a part of my morning devotionals. Do you know what it says?"

With a shake of her head, she waited.

"'For the gifts and the calling of God are irrevocable.'"

The intensity of his eyes anchored her to him. "For the first time ever, I really understood what people meant by having an epiphany. It was like parts of my brain opened and God's words filled it. I might've gotten off His path, but God kept righting me."

His eyes glowed with excitement. "I had been given the most precious gift, and then it was multiplied. God's been working on me even if I didn't trust Him the way I should."

He sighed. "You're a gift that can't be revoked or replaced. By turning you away, I *was* being a coward. Telling God I didn't trust His word."

With her thumb she wiped the single tear that had fallen from his eye.

He caught her hand and held it there. "Five years ago, I committed my life to serving Christ. When you came back with Rosie, I was overwhelmed and dealing with new emotions. I have a hard enough time dealing with the old ones. I didn't know what to do, so I waited for something bad to happen instead of accepting the gift and treasuring it like I should have. I failed you again."

She needed space to process all his beautiful words. Breaking contact, she went to her desk.

He joined her. Not getting too close, he held out his hand. She didn't hesitate. One hand in his, she picked up a ceramic starfish painted with the exuberance of a three-year-old who loved purple. It had been a Christmas gift from Rosie.

Squeezing Elijah's hand, she looked him in the eye. "One starfish at a time or one day at a time. We can make a difference. I want to make a difference in Port Del Mar. With you. I wanted to honor—"

He crushed her to him, holding her so close it was difficult for air to get in her lungs.

His lips pressed against her ear. "I love you so much. I love you. I should have told you that sooner, but I'm saying it now and I want to say it every day. I can move to Denver if you want." His hold on her relaxed. He moved his lips to the corner of her forehead. "But, honestly, I want you and Rosie to come back to Port Del Mar. Come home and let us figure out our future." Hands slid down her arms, fingers entwining with hers, then flexing. "Please, don't let go of me."

She wrapped her arms around him. "You're mine. I'm not giving you back. I love you, Elijah De La Rosa. I always have, and I always will."

They might have messed up the first time, but it had shaped them into the people they were now. With God's grace they would figure out the future, of that she had no doubt.

Epilogue

Elijah adjusted the red scarf and flipped the bead-covered dreadlocks over his shoulder. Lane needed a raise for wearing this for every pirate trip. The boat swayed.

For the hundredth time, his hand went to his pocket. The ring was still there. This time he was asking with her parents' blessing. They would be here with his family and all the families in Rosie's first grade class.

He had to get this right. But he was having major doubts about the plan. He'd been dragging his feet, wanting it to be perfect, but the need to tuck Rosemarie into her bedroom at his house, their home, was driving him crazy.

"Daddy!" The reason he was wearing this ridiculous get-up wrapped her arms around his neck. Zoe, the doll he had given her on their first meeting, had a red bandanna wrapped around her black curly hair. "I knew you were a real pirate." She giggled and climbed into his lap and started playing with the colorful beads in the wig.

"Where's your mom?"

"She and GiGi are doing last-minute stuff. Papa brought me, so I can help you."

He chuckled. Jazmine had always been good at managing people without them even knowing.

"So, do I get a sword?" Judge Daniels joined them.

"Yes!" She slid down and pulled two plastic swords from a barrel. "This is going to be the best day ever." She jumped in place. "Daddy! You're doing it, right? For my birthday."

"Doing what?" her grandfather asked, as he pretended to be stabbed.

Elijah sighed and eyed his daughter. "For her birthday she only wants one thing from me."

Rosie twirled. "I want Daddy to marry Mommy for my birthday. I always wanted a sister, but that takes more time if you don't order ahead."

The Judge laughed, and some of the tension drained from Elijah's shoulders.

Standing, he picked up his daughter. "Crazy idea, right?"

"Asking Jazmine to marry you?" The older

man crossed his arms and leaned on the edge of the faux ship. "Or proposing at a six-year-old's pirate party?"

His father-in-law sat down and propped his deck shoes on a short barrel. "This is going to be a great show. You can't back out now, boy. Lea told me she gave you my mother's ring. You got it?"

"Yes, sir." His throat went dry.

"Good." He winked. "Girls like that kind of thing. And I can tell you from experience that telling your daughter no never gets easier."

"Elijah!" Jazz called from below.

"Yes?" He went to the edge. Jazmine stood on the dock, boxes of cupcakes and a bundle of flowers in her arms.

"My mom needs help unloading the car," she called up to him.

"Got it."

That was the last moment not swamped in controlled chaos.

As they pulled away from the dock, he watched Jazz laughing and interacting with everyone.

Several times she caught him staring and smiled at him. Occasionally he worked his way over to her to steal a quick kiss. Like any good pirate would do.

The afternoon flew. The sun was setting,

and they were heading back to the dock. It was time.

The young second mate distracted everyone with an outrageous song, so Elijah had time to climb up the platform. He unhooked the rope.

This might be the worst idea he had ever had while sober.

Lane winked up at him, then made his move. Drawing his plastic sword, the second mate held it to Jazmine's throat and told her he would be taking all her jewelry. The kids screamed and ran to her rescue. But the crew held the kids back, and they all laughed as they played along.

Jazmine looked confused. Her gaze searched the boat. She was looking for him.

"Argh!" he roared, and jumped from the platform, swinging across the deck. His boots landed on the box anchored to the floor specifically for this scene, one they usually played out for tourists.

The kids and parents cheered. His sister might have been the loudest. "Hands off the lady, you scoundrel!" Elijah used his best pirate voice.

Lane turned, and they lunged back and forth, slashing at each other with their plastic swords. Backed into the corner, Lane went to his knees and surrendered. He might have done a bit of overacting, but the kids loved it.

Dramatically, Elijah sheathed his sword. Swaggering across the deck to where Jazmine stood, he took her in his arms. For a moment he stopped and looked into her eyes. This might be over the top, but he wanted her to see him. To see the love he had for her.

Slowly, he lowered his head and kissed her as hoots and hollers surrounded them. Pulling back, he grinned at her.

Smiling, she raised her eyebrows. "What if this lady plans on saving herself?"

He removed his leather gauntlet and cupped her face. Leaning in, he kissed her nose. "She is more than capable, but this is what our daughter wanted. And I wanted you, so it works out." He winked, then twisted to face Lane. "Bring in the treasure so we can share our bounty."

The shrieks were higher than his ears could gauge as Lane and Carlos carried a wooden chest onto the deck. Elijah kneeled before the ancient-looking lock and, with a flourish, broke it. A hush fell over the kiddie crowd. The water hitting the sides of the boat was the only sound heard.

He lifted the lid. On top of the costume jewelry, chocolate coins and brightly colored beads sat a small velvet box. Closing his fist over it and pressing it to his chest, he turned on his heel and strode over to the love of his life.

She tilted her head, her eyes narrowed. He grinned. This would be something they would always remember. This was a good plan. He hoped.

One of the dreadlocks dropped across his face, and he yanked off the wig and bandanna. He wanted this to be real.

Her fingers went to his hair, trying to bring some sort of order to it.

In front of her, he dropped to one knee. She gasped.

"I've asked you before, and I broke those vows." He swallowed against the dryness of his throat. "You have no reason other than faith to be my wife again. Life without you is nothing but a gray mist. You fill every day with beautiful color. I want to give you all the love you deserve." He lifted the box and offered her the ring. "Will you marry me again?"

Her hands pressed against her mouth. "That's… That's…" Her eyes flashed to her mother before coming back to him. "You have Mama CiCi's ring." Slowly she went to her knees in front of him.

Her hand cupped his. Her eyes stayed on him. "What took you so long?" Her voice was low and hoarse. Tears glistened in the kindest eyes he had ever looked into.

"I wanted to make it perfect."

Tears overflowed her dark lashes. "I've never much liked perfect. I love you and our life together. Yes, I'll marry you as many times as you ask."

He slipped the ring onto her finger where it belonged. It felt like going home again, but this time with the support and love of their families. Standing, he pulled her up with him and brushed his lips against hers.

A small body slammed into them. "Are you married now?"

They laughed. "No, sweetheart. We're engaged."

"When can we move in with Daddy? I want a puppy and a baby sister."

He swung his daughter up against his shoulder. "Give us a little time, sweet girl. You get to help your mom plan a wedding."

With a nod, Jazz kissed Rosie's cheek. "A very small wedding that will take less than a few weeks to organize."

He slipped his hand into the woman's who had always owned his heart. Lane and Carlos passed out the loot and the party favors. They docked, the families chatting as they disembarked. By the time the sun slipped out of the sky, his family stood alone on the deck.

Belle hugged him and whispered in his ear, "I'm so happy for you. You're the best guy, and you deserve to be happy."

"So do you, sis."

Stepping back, she shook her head. "I am happy. Now that you have your wife back, don't start matchmaking."

Selena laughed. Holding one of the triplets, she leaned in for a hug, too. "Don't worry, I've got the perfect guy for her." She laughed at the horror on Belle's face.

Azalea helped with the other two triplets as they made their way off the ship. With just the string of party lights breaking the shadows of night, Elijah stood with his soon-to-be wife again and his daughter, and waved goodbye to everyone.

For a moment he wanted to fall to his knees and thank God for a life he had never even dared to dream of.

Rosie's eyes fluttered shut, and her head fell against his shoulder. Jazz pressed her cheek to his other shoulder and sighed.

With a yawn, Rosie snuggled closer to him. "Who knew life on a fake pirate ship could be so perfect?"

He kissed the top of her head. "Stick with

me, babe, and the adventures will only get better. I love you."

"I love you, too, Daddy." The sleepy voice interrupted his thoughts. "Now that we're engaged, are we going home with you?"

"Not tonight, sweetheart, but soon. Very soon I'll take you home."

He felt Jazz's smile as her hand went to Rosemarie's back. "It won't be long before we'll be going home together."

His heart clenched, and he tightened his arms around his world, holding them close. He had been waiting for them, and he would be taking them home soon.

Jazmine stretched to her toes and kissed his cheek. "Elijah De La Rosa, you're my home. I love you, always will."

His hand in hers and his daughter on his shoulder, they walked the plank. Together.

* * * * *

If you enjoyed this story, look for these other books by Jolene Navarro available now.

Texas Daddy
The Texan's Twins
Lone Star Christmas

Dear Reader,

Welcome to Port Del Mar. I'm excited to start a new series and hope you enjoyed meeting the De La Rosa family. I have fallen in love with them all.

Stories of redemption and forgiveness (accepting and giving) have always reached out to me.

As I started traveling the road with Elijah and Jazmine, I realized this was not going to be an easy journey to write.

Alcoholism and running with a child are heavy subject matters that I don't take lightly. I prayed as the words formed their story. People make mistakes, and I truly believe God can change a person.

Elijah and Jazmine had to seek God first in order to make the future they wanted work. With each page I loved them even more.

If you know of anyone who needs help with alcoholism, they can reach out to Alcoholics Anonymous at www.aa.org or for those who are affected by a loved one's drinking behavior visit the Al-Anon Family Group at al-anon.org.

I hope you come back to Port Del Mar to read Selena's story.

Many blessings,
Jolene Navarro

Get 4 FREE REWARDS!

We'll send you 2 FREE Books plus 2 FREE Mystery Gifts.

Love Inspired® Suspense books feature Christian characters facing challenges to their faith... and lives.

FREE
Value Over
$20

YES! Please send me 2 FREE Love Inspired® Suspense novels and my 2 FREE mystery gifts (gifts are worth about $10 retail). After receiving them, if I don't wish to receive any more books, I can return the shipping statement marked "cancel." If I don't cancel, I will receive 4 brand-new novels every month and be billed just $5.24 each for the regular-print edition or $5.74 each for the larger-print edition in the U.S., or $5.74 each for the regular-print edition or $6.24 each for the larger-print edition in Canada. That's a savings of at least 13% off the cover price. It's quite a bargain! Shipping and handling is just 50¢ per book in the U.S. and 75¢ per book in Canada.* I understand that accepting the 2 free books and gifts places me under no obligation to buy anything. I can always return a shipment and cancel at any time. The free books and gifts are mine to keep no matter what I decide.

Choose one: ☐ **Love Inspired® Suspense**
Regular-Print
(153/353 IDN GMY5)

☐ **Love Inspired® Suspense**
Larger-Print
(107/307 IDN GMY5)

Name (please print)

Address   Apt. #

City   State/Province   Zip/Postal Code

Mail to the **Reader Service:**
IN U.S.A.: P.O. Box 1341, Buffalo, NY 14240-8531
IN CANADA: P.O. Box 603, Fort Erie, Ontario L2A 5X3

Want to try 2 free books from another series! Call 1-800-873-8635 or visit www.ReaderService.com.

*Terms and prices subject to change without notice. Prices do not include sales taxes, which will be charged (if applicable) based on your state or country of residence. Canadian residents will be charged applicable taxes. Offer not valid in Quebec. This offer is limited to one order per household. Books received may not be as shown. Not valid for current subscribers to Love Inspired Suspense books. All orders subject to approval. Credit or debit balances in a customer's account(s) may be offset by any other outstanding balance owed by or to the customer. Please allow 4 to 6 weeks for delivery. Offer available while quantities last.

Your Privacy—The Reader Service is committed to protecting your privacy. Our Privacy Policy is available online at www.ReaderService.com or upon request from the Reader Service. We make a portion of our mailing list available to reputable third parties that offer products we believe may interest you. If you prefer that we not exchange your name with third parties, or if you wish to clarify or modify your communication preferences, please visit us at www.ReaderService.com/consumerschoice or write to us at Reader Service Preference Service, P.O. Box 9062, Buffalo, NY 14240-9062. Include your complete name and address.

LIS19R2

Get 4 FREE REWARDS!

We'll send you 2 FREE Books plus 2 FREE Mystery Gifts.

Harlequin® Heartwarming™ Larger-Print books feature traditional values of home, family, community and—most of all—love.

FREE Value Over $20

YES! Please send me 2 FREE Harlequin® Heartwarming™ Larger-Print novels and my 2 FREE mystery gifts (gifts worth about $10 retail). After receiving them, if I don't wish to receive any more books, I can return the shipping statement marked "cancel." If I don't cancel, I will receive 4 brand-new larger-print novels every month and be billed just $5.49 per book in the U.S. or $6.24 per book in Canada. That's a savings of at least 19% off the cover price. It's quite a bargain! Shipping and handling is just 50¢ per book in the U.S. and 75¢ per book in Canada.* I understand that accepting the 2 free books and gifts places me under no obligation to buy anything. I can always return a shipment and cancel at any time. The free books and gifts are mine to keep no matter what I decide.

161/361 IDN GMY3

Name (please print)

Address   Apt. #

City   State/Province   Zip/Postal Code

Mail to the **Reader Service:**
IN U.S.A.: P.O. Box 1341, Buffalo, NY 14240-8531
IN CANADA: P.O. Box 603, Fort Erie, Ontario L2A 5X3

Want to try 2 free books from another series! Call 1-800-873-8635 or visit www.ReaderService.com.

---

*Terms and prices subject to change without notice. Prices do not include sales taxes, which will be charged (if applicable) based on your state or country of residence. Canadian residents will be charged applicable taxes. Offer not valid in Quebec. This offer is limited to one order per household. Books received may not be as shown. Not valid for current subscribers to Harlequin Heartwarming Larger-Print books. All orders subject to approval. Credit or debit balances in a customer's account(s) may be offset by any other outstanding balance owed by or to the customer. Please allow 4 to 6 weeks for delivery. Offer available while quantities last.

Your Privacy—The Reader Service is committed to protecting your privacy. Our Privacy Policy is available online at www.ReaderService.com or upon request from the Reader Service. We make a portion of our mailing list available to reputable third parties that offer products we believe may interest you. If you prefer that we not exchange your name with third parties, or if you wish to clarify or modify your communication preferences, please visit us at www.ReaderService.com/consumerschoice or write to us at Reader Service Preference Service, P.O. Box 9062, Buffalo, NY 14240-9062. Include your complete name and address.

HW19R2